GHOSTLIKE

Andy Merriman is the biographer of Hattie Jacques (*Hattie*) and Margaret Rutherford (*Dreadnought with Good Manners*) and the author of *A Minor Adjustment* and *A Major Adjustment*, about his daughter who has Down's syndrome, and *Greasepaint and Cordite*, a history of entertainment in World War II. He has ghostwritten a number of books, including *My Story*, although Basil Brush claims to have written it himself.

GHOSTLIKE

A novel

ANDY MERRIMAN

First published 2025 by Palace Books

Copyright © Andy Merriman 2025

Andy Merriman has asserted his moral right to be identified as the Author
of this Work in accordance with the Copyright Designs and Patents Act 1988.

All rights reserved.

No part of this book may be reproduced or utilised in any form
or by any means, electronic or mechanical, including photocopying,
recording or by any information storage and retrieval system,
without permission in writing from Palace Books.

Every effort has been made to trace the copyright holders
of material quoted in this book. If application is made in writing
to the publisher, any omissions will be included in future editions.

A catalogue record for this book
is available from the British Library.

Typeset in 11 pt on 16 pt Filosofia by M Rules Ltd

In memory of Christopher Forbes Merriman

A woman lies in a hospital bed. She has an itch which she can't scratch. She can hear a fly buzzing around her head. She would love to swat it, but she can't. A tracheostomy, which allows her to breathe, and a gastric tube providing nourishment, have been part of her for six months. She is desperate for a glass of wine, a glass of water, a glass of anything. She can't speak or move. Only, her eyes can blink — furiously at times, slowly at others. She is, perhaps, in her fifties, but it is difficult to tell as all that can be seen of her is her pale face and greying, tousled hair.

Two nurses enter the room. In unison they gently turn the patient onto her side. One of them squeezes her hand. 'All right, darling?'

There is no response.

They tuck the patient in and at the doorway, out of the patient's hearing, one nurse shakes her head and looks at her colleague. 'Sometimes I wonder if . . .'

'I know. I know.'

Soon afterwards a masked figure in green scrubs enters the side room swiftly, closing the door behind him. He leans over the woman, nods, and reaches for a pillow from under her head. He lowers the surgical mask to press his face close to hers and whisper something to her. She stares up at him, her eyes following his movements.

The figure places the pillow over the woman's face and presses it firmly for a couple of minutes.

Once he has checked her eyes are closed he replaces the pillow under her head. At the doorway he pauses to look back. Then he replaces his mask and closes the door behind him.

1

Nick Greenwood re-read the text for the umpteenth time. Why would his GP be urging him to make an appointment? Why couldn't they tell him the results of the blood test over the phone? Surely every man of his age had the odd problem with his waterworks? An automatically generated text: that must be it. Put it out of your mind. Just another close shave. It will be OK.

It was actually surprising that Nick was still alive. His maternal grandmother, discovering to her horror that she was pregnant at the age of 44, had taken an overdose of Epsom salts. She'd had severe stomach pains, but a healthy baby. Some 25 years later his own mother, realizing *she* was pregnant, had taken a knife to her abdomen. Fortunately for Nick no blood was spilt other than a slight graze to Mrs Greenwood's thumb. Applying some witch-hazel, Nick's father had wondered why such a minor injury had made his wife so tearful.

There had been other brushes with death. When Nick was five, he had wandered close to the precipice at Beachy Head. This time his now devoted mother had kept calm, and lured him back with sweets. He had nurtured a fondness for wine gums ever since. In his twenties there had been a 'bad trip', when he had jumped out of a window thinking he was Icarus. Or was it Douglas Bader? In his thirties there had been a hurried exit from a love nest at the hands of a cuckolded Nigerian boxer; a decade later, an unfortunate 'sit-on' mower incident while attempting to cut his father's grass. But now, at the age of 64, he was still in the land of the living. Or at least a cramped, untidy flat in Chalk Farm.

Nick had survived Covid, but had continued to wear a mask long after it was mandatory, having known several people succumb to the pandemic. During the first lockdowns Nick had stood outside his flat and clapped NHS staff. Indeed, so enthusiastic had he been banging his special saucepan in support of medics and caregivers that he had broken a wooden spoon. Then he had hurried inside for fear of having to chat with neighbours — Nick had read that Covid had brought on neighbourliness. Pre-Covid, someone had arrived on his doorstep to announce a street party. 'I'd rather stick needles in my eyes,' he declared.

'I'll take that as a no,' she replied. A few days later he found a package outside his front door. It contained a T-shirt with 'Street Curmudgeon' emblazoned across the chest.

Fair play, Nick thought. At least I got a free T-shirt I can wear with pride.

And after obeying all the regulations, taken all the precautions, endured all the endless lockdowns, the boredom, the exhausting Zoom meetings — this. It seemed a bit unfair.

Nick flipped his laptop open, for once ignoring the lure of Twitter, his Fantasy Football Team score and generous offers from West African princes. *'As the sunlight cast mysterious shadows on the dappled meadow ahead'*, he read, *'and pipits sang gloriously as if warning their young that cuckoos had just flown in from Africa, I realised that summer . . .'*

He screwed his eyes up. Had he written this? In which case whose book was it?

Didn't sound like Frankie Morrison – unless the rock guitarist had suddenly developed an interest in birdwatching. Could it be the former gangster Charlie Robertson, now living the bucolic life in Essex? Or the international footballer-turned-Sky pundit Junior Hamilton? Nope. Nick couldn't place it. He set about scrolling through other projects he'd been working on recently.

He'd imagined a career brighter than this. Since brief success in 1979 with his first novel, then several biographies for which his agent had managed to sell the film rights, he'd been reduced to writing gags for long-forgotten Radio 4 sketch shows and the odd radio play – and now he was reduced to ghostwriting the autobiographies of little-known celebrities. Some weren't even that. Every one of them was convinced of possessing a wealth of 'hilarious' stories and anecdotes that would make a bestseller.

These days, therefore, Nick occasionally distracted himself. To alleviate some of the tedium of the work he set himself the challenge of getting certain favourite words into his daily target – even if it sometimes went against the elementary rule of ghostwriting: that of capturing the voice of the subject. 'Solipsistic' was a frequent candidate. So were 'crepuscular' and 'alchemy'. In fact, he had managed to get them into most of his 19 books.

'Fine words butter no parsnips' was also a sentence that seemed to find its way in. It had an elegiac tenor – 'elegiac' was another word that elevated him from 'hack' to legitimate writer, although he had had difficulty including it in Junior Hamilton's autobiography, *Settling Scores*.

Most mornings he began by checking his reviews on Amazon. Although mainly positive, there were some which inevitably caused him some consternation. Nick was particularly peeved by criticism and star scores that had nothing to do with him – he had received one star for a book that had arrived later than expected. Other verdicts struck closer to home. 'This book could have been much improved if he had employed a ghostwriter,' for example. Or, 'This biography by Greenwood should have been written when Pomponio Algerio was alive.' The Italian martyr had been boiled in oil in 1556.

The door of his study burst open. It was his son, Ben. 'Dad, Grace needs someone to keep an eye on Marcel.'

'Now?'

'Just for an hour.'

Nick raised his hands in a gesture of helplessness. 'I've got a meeting with Frankie Morrison.'

'Dad . . . She never asks for help unless she really has to.'

'Um . . . tell you what: tell Grace you'll look after Marcel.'

'What about my essay?'

'When's it due?'

'Two weeks ago.'

'Please, Ben. Marcel loves you.'

Ben sighed. 'OK, OK! I'll go.'

For a 21-year-old, Ben was surprisingly prone to guilt. Nick worried that his son sometimes carried the weight of the world on his shoulders, so determined was he to make the world a fairer place. Given half a chance he would have joined the young man who stopped the tanks in Tiananmen Square.

'But if I get in trouble with my tutor . . .'

'Don't let Marcel win,' Nick called out just before the slam of the front door. 'That would be patronising.'

'Anything?'

'Not having one of my best days.'

'Come on, Frankie. I need *something*.'

The man opposite, bejewelled, thin as a twig and dressed in black leather trousers, an inky linen jacket and cowboy boots, scratched his charcoal-dyed ringlets.

A small digital recorder sat on the table between them, but Nick was poised with pen and pad. He was what some people described as a 'belt-and-braces' man. Frankie's face was contorted with effort. They were seated in the Canal Hotel, a Little Venice pub and music venue that had also seen better days. The crystal chandeliers, stained-glass windows and grand marble fireplace remained, but so did the tatty scarlet velvet curtains falling to the mosaic floor, the ripped flock wallpaper and the red banquettes from which flecks of yellow foam burst among the blackened cigarette burns. Frankie drained his third vodka and orange and leaned back in his leather armchair. 'Nah.' He paused for effect. 'You know I could have been one of the Stones?'

'You told me. Were it not for Keith.' Nick smiled weakly and finished his third pint of Special. 'And Brian Jones.' He turned over the blank page of his notebook. 'You played here, didn't you?'

'If you say so.'

'I do say so. You forgot to tell me. I found an old *Melody Maker* press cutting on the Internet. One of your first bands played with Moosehead Williams in nineteen sixty-five. Listen: "*Acclaimed American bluesman Moosehead Williams wowed fans last night in the basement venue of the Canal Boat. Backed by able English band Aslan's Roar, Moosehead was in fine fettle and performed a number of his hits, although he was clearly unhappy with the guitarist, Frankie Morton.*"'

'Bloody hell! They couldn't even get my name right! Yeah, he was horrible.'

'Anything else about the gig?'

'*Horrible.*'

A dishevelled man wearing what appeared to be an orange sock on his head and matching shorts, even though it was deep into winter, was approaching. 'Hey, man, you're not Frankie Morrison, are you? Me and Den over there' – a pony-tailed man sitting at the bar proffered a double thumbs-up – 'we love your music. We are *literally* your greatest fans. We wondered if it was you, but you look older in real life.'

Delight competed with irritation on Frankie's face. Fans were fans and you had to be cool with them. 'Yes, that's me.' He chuckled throatily. 'Last time I looked.' It was not the first time he had used this witticism.

'Unbelievable! My lucky day! Can we buy you a drink?'

Before Nick could step in Frankie had nodded. 'My lucky day too.'

'I'm Dave. Den, Frankie wants us to join him! What you drinking, Frankie?' Dave turned to Nick. 'And what about you?'

'I'm all right, thanks. Look, Frankie, we're trying to do some work here.'

'I'm writing a book,' Frankie told his new best friend. 'This is my mate Nick, who's helping a bit. It's ... cathartic,' he went on.

'We saw you here with Moosehead Williams.' His mate had joined them at the table with three drinks. 'Here, Den, I was just telling Frankie we saw him here.'

'Great gig. This is unbelievable, by the way.' Den was genuinely emotional. 'One of the best days of my life.'

'Wait a minute.' Nick sat straight up. 'You were both here?'

'One of the best gigs we've ever been to. Eh, Den?'

Den nodded sagely. 'That Moosehead was a right cunt. He had a go at you when you missed an intro.'

Nick switched on the recorder and broke open his pad. 'You saw lots of their performances?'

Dave was triumphant. 'We were the band's greatest fans.'

Nick scribbled notes and Frankie sat back beaming while Dave and Den rattled on about the crowd, the set list, the other members of the band, what guitar he was playing that night.

Half an hour and a couple of drinks later, the two fans were starting to repeat themselves. 'Well, this has been great, guys. Thanks so much.'

'We've got lots more,' said Dave, crestfallen. 'Haven't we, Den?'

'I think we have enough for now. We'll put you in the acknowledgements.'

Dave and Den returned reluctantly to their bar stools. Frankie called over, 'It's been great, fellas!'

Nick was genuinely grateful. 'OK. Nineteen eighty-six?'

'Nineteen eighty-six.'

Nick edged the digital recorder a little closer. 'You were meant to be opening for Ozzie Osbourne.'

Frankie scratched his nose. 'Nineteen . . . eighty . . . six?

'You'd just married Frenchie Murdock.'

Frankie's eyes lit up like a joint. 'Oh, yeah. She was something else.'

'You were married. For a month and a half.' Nick looked expectantly at Frankie.

'As long as that? Nineteen eighty-six?'

'And you began work on the first Dog's Breath album. Or you were meant to.'

'Was that nineteen eighty-six? Sold millions of albums, you know.'

'I know. Come on, Frankie.'

Frankie pondered some more, then raised his hand as if hailing a taxi. 'Hang on, man. Nineteen eighty-six. Yeah. *Yeah* –yeah, I remember nineteen eighty-six. Yeah, course. Like yesterday. Bloody hell.'

Nick had never seen Frankie so animated, 'Go on.'

Frankie stared at Nick, eyes bright with triumph. 'The *Challenger*.'

'What?'

'The Space Shuttle *Challenger*. Big fucking rocket. Just blew the fuck up. January nineteen eighty-six!'

Nick felt weary beyond speech. 'Right. Of course. You see, the idea, Frankie, is that you tell me stuff that's, well . . . personal. Pertinent to you. And the band. I mean, the *Challenger* was just a news story, wasn't it? It was a story.'

'Pretty fucking big story! It's like when Kennedy was shot. Everyone remembers where they were when Kennedy was shot.'

'And do you remember where you were when the *Challenger* blew up?'

Frankie, lost in thought, took a moment to process this. 'Oh. Yeah.' He smiled mischievously. 'I was in bed with those two girls off breakfast TV.'

Nick sank his head to his chest. He'd had enough of this. 'Yes, you've told me about them. At least we've got a date for that now.' He turned off the recorder. 'We'll do this again next week, OK? Why don't you put your name into YouTube, see if anything jogs your memory?'

Frankie looked disappointed he wouldn't be able to tell his three-in-a-bed story again, so Nick suggested he go and join Dave and Den, who'd been looking over expectantly.

'Yeah, I'll do that. I'll see what else they know about me.'

'What a g-goal! That was a g-goal! I'm winning!' Marcel punched the air and ran around the sitting room, hands raised heavenwards.

'Marcel, you've done it again.'

'No, it's a g-goal.'

'You scored in the wrong end.'

Marcel stopped celebrating, 'No. C-c-can't be.'

'Well, look at the score.' Ben indicated the television screen. 'Tottenham nil, Manchester United five.'

'It's wrong. Man . . . ches . . . ter' – Marcel couldn't quite pronounce 'Manchester' – 'are rubbish.'

'Try the pass button, not the shoot button if you're passing back to the goalie. But best to try and kick the other way.'

Marcel looked confused, before his expression turned to frustration. 'I'm a little bit useless.'

'No, you're not. It's only twenty minutes gone. You've got time to come back. Come on, your kick-off.'

Marcel's mood shifted immediately. 'I love FIFA!'

Ben heard a key in the lock.

'M-mum!' Marcel threw down his handset and rushed to the door, nearly knocking his mother over. 'I'm winning! I'm beating Ben again! I'm a good player, Mum.'

Grace smiled. 'Yes, you are. Has he been behaving himself?'

Ben nodded. 'Of course.'

'Come on, Ben, let's do another game. This one's completely wrong. P-*please*!' Marcel grabbed Ben around the waist.

'Marcel, you must let Ben go.' Grace gave her son 'the look'.

'Is your m-mum m-making you go too, Ben?'

Ben hesitated. 'No . . .'

Marcel looked puzzled. 'I never met your mum.'

'That's because . . . It's difficult to explain.' Ben looked at Grace.

'Leave Ben alone, Marcel. Thanks, Ben. I'm sorry I had to dash off.'

'Don't worry. I enjoy playing on the PlayStation with Marcel – even though he always beats me.' Ben winked.

'That's 'cos you're rubbish.' Marcel laughed at his own joke.

'Bit of an emergency. I have this client who's applied for asylum and the Home Office are being difficult.'

'Well, I think all borders are racist.' Ben waited eagerly for Grace's affirmation.

'That's one way of looking at it.'

'That's exactly what my dad said. He said he agreed in principle but wasn't sure about the practicalities. He's obsessed with practicalities.'

'How is your dad?'

Ben wondered why Grace always asked after his dad. He supposed he was likeable in his own way. He wondered why his dad had never made a play for Grace, whom he'd once described as a Denise Lewis lookalike. Ben didn't know exactly who Denise Lewis was – all he knew was Grace was pretty stylish, clever, and he even allowed himself to think of her as 'fit'. Ben liked her direct approach, and she was brilliant with Marcel.

Perhaps his dad had made a move and been rejected – although Grace did seem to have developed a bit of a soft spot for him over the years they'd been neighbours. Ben liked having Grace and Marcel living in the upstairs flat; anything romantic would alter the whole dynamic. Not something to dwell on.

'He's OK. Gone for another meeting with a client, or maybe his therapist. Although I'm not meant to know about that.' Ben paused. 'You're probably not meant to know either.' He shrugged. 'Dad likes getting out of the flat. Apparently the life of a writer is very lonely.'

Nick had decided to walk home along the Regent's Canal. Thanks to Den and Dave he reckoned he'd got a few more pages on Frankie. Opposite the Feng Shang Princess, the 'floating' Chinese restaurant in the Cumberland Spur, he'd been approached by a woman selling the *Big Issue*. When Nick reached into his pocket for some change the woman's eyes lit up. 'My last copy.'

'Oh, good,' Nick said. 'Now you can go home.'

The woman stared at Nick in stunned silence. 'I'm homeless, you *moron*. That's why I'm selling the *Big Issue*.'

'I'm so sorry – I didn't mean to be – can I give you double for the paper?' Nick delved into his pocket for some more change but only came up with a tenner, which he quickly tried to hide.

'That'll do.' The woman held out her hand.

'Ah. I didn't mean to give you that much. Could you give me six pounds back, then—?' But the woman was already off.

His phone bleeped with a new text. *My son calls another man Daddy.*

Nick's heart sank. That was all he needed. Whenever his dad communicated in song titles it meant he was in a chatty mood.

Richard Greenwood was a retired art dealer and had once owned a gallery in Mayfair. He'd had been evacuated to a Suffolk village during the war and had always held a soft spot for the county's forgiving landscapes and dramatic panoramas, and following the loss of his wife ten years previously had retired to the very same village.

Reluctantly Nick rang back. 'Hi Dad, how are you?'

'I just called to say I love you.'

'Dad, can we quit the song lyrics? I really don't have the time.'

'Don't get around much any more.'

'*Dad!*'

'All right, all right. I think I've found you another subject.'

'Thanks, Dad, but I've got far too much on as it is.'

'He lives in my village. It's a very interesting story. He's discovered—'

'Look, I just can't take on any more work. I appreciate you thinking of me, but I'm up to my ears. Everything else all right?'

'Yes, fine, although I did have a little fall yesterday. Well, I'd describe it as more of a trip . . .'

The conversation added to Nick's concern about his father. On his last visit to Suffolk he had discovered a button mushroom stuffed into the top of his father's hot water bottle. 'I'm not going doolally — it's just my eyesight that isn't so good.' And Richard had been using two half-empty boxes of tissues as footwear, on the grounds that 'they're more comfortable than my slippers.' In the future his dad was only likely to become more reliant on him. It was the burden of being 'an only child' — Nick still never knew when to confess to this much maligned status. Every trait of his was apparently down to having no brothers or sisters. Shyness, selfishness, an inability to share, a need for solitude — everything was attributed to a lack of siblings.

For six months, however, technically he hadn't been an only child, and 50 years later still wasn't sure whether to describe himself as one or not. He still had vivid, shocking memories:

eight years old, playing Subbuteo with a friend, his mother running into the sitting room with a baby in her arms screaming hysterically, '*He's dead! He's dead. My baby's dead!*' Richard had ordered Nick and his friend upstairs, and soon afterwards both his parents, stricken and pale, had come into his bedroom with the news that his baby brother Christopher had suffocated in his cot. His name was barely ever mentioned again by his grieving parents.

The following day Nick had been called into the headmaster's study at the minor prep school he attended. Thinking he had done something wrong by copying Roger Baker's homework, he was relieved to be told by the Revd Thompson, 'Try to think of it as your brother being too good for this world.' Nick's schoolmates were too young to express sympathy. Paul Jacobs did offer him the future loan of his Airfix Spitfire model, Jonny Downing offered his last black wine gum, and Toby Shooter had given him the Dinky E-type Jag he always kept in his blazer pocket – gestures Nick had never forgotten.

2

The offices of Philpott, Sellers and Hill, literary agents, occupied the ground floor of a Georgian townhouse coincidentally located in the same street in Soho where one of Nick's ancestors, George Fry, MP and escapologist, had lived in 1832 – a fact he never tired of telling anyone at the agency. Some Edwardian counterpart of Laurence Llewelyn-Bowen had decided that the remaining period features should be stripped out; photographs of the agency's more successful clients covered the walls of reception. Seeing his face missing, Nick had sent in a portrait of his that, with his silver hair brushed back from a slightly receding hairline above horn-rimmed glasses, made him look a little like a young Bill Nighy. He'd even had the photograph framed, and ignored the query from the receptionist as to whether the subject was one of their clients. The portrait was never seen again.

'Can I help you?' The new receptionist seemed equally ignorant of Nick's existence.

'Nick Greenwood.'

'Yes?'

'I'm here to see Clarissa.'

'Which one?'

Of course there had to be more than one Clarissa. There were probably a handful. And many more in literary agencies and publishers all over London. And all mid-twenties and oblivious of any authors over 40. 'Clarissa Watson-Brown.'

'Is she expecting you?'

'Yes, she's expecting me. My agent is actually Graham Sellers, but—'

'He's in Mauritius. Take a seat.'

'Any chance of a coffee?'

'I don't do that.'

'Of course you don't.' Nick regarded the impossibly low leather couch and said he would rather stand.

The young woman looked disconcerted. 'As long as you'll be all right.'

Fifteen minutes later, Nick had been forced to take a seat with a severe attack of cramp in his left calf, when Clarissa appeared. 'Oh, hi, Nick. Super to see you. Follow me.' Nick heaved himself off the couch with an over-exaggerated flourish.

There was an air of confidence and self-satisfaction about Clarissa Watson-Brown that Nick had always found annoying and yet enviable. Although still in her mid-twenties, she exuded the air of someone who knew everything about everything. The sort of person who would even enjoy her own company, which was a boon for her as nobody else did. Her looks helped: sylph-like, sharply dressed, a mass of tame auburn hair, which she tossed every minute on the minute, and dazzling, laser-like blue eyes that could slice cheese. She had once auditioned for *Made in Chelsea* but been rejected as too 'self-centred'.

In the meeting room everything was chrome. Clarissa made herself comfortable at the head of the table. She was pretty clueless about Nick's work and had never heard of most of his subjects. She didn't really see why she had to deal with him at all when there were interns bright enough to handle him. He wasn't really considered a proper writer: just telling someone else's story, not creating his own. Clarissa had also become frustrated at his inability to come to terms with social media. In her view he was lucky to obtain an advance at all.

'Junior not here yet?' Nick wanted to make the point that he had been professionally punctual.

'You know what he's like.'

Nick did. In the three years he had spent working with Junior, there had only been one occasion when Junior had actually been on time, and that was because he needed Nick's urgent help in procuring a visa. Footballers usually had that sort of thing taken care of by their club. It wasn't that Junior couldn't sort it out – he was actually one of Nick's brightest subjects; he'd just become dependent on Nick for all sorts of assistance. In fact, Nick had discovered through his work as a ghostwriter that he could be called upon as a personal assistant, marital counsellor, life coach and even psychotherapist.

'So. How are things going with – what's his name ...? Frankie ...' She paused. 'Frankie Morrison?' Clarissa was pleased she had remembered the name of one of Nick's troublesome subjects.

'Like getting blood out of a non-Rolling Stone.' Nick waited for Clarissa to laugh, or at least smile. 'Brain's gone. I don't know how I'm going to get a book out of him.'

To be fair to him, the autobiography hadn't been Frankie's idea. The fading rock star's manager had thought it would put his client's career back on track. 'It took us months just to agree a title,' Nick went on. His idea had been much better: *Riffing Yarns*. But Frankie had refused to do the book unless it was called *Four Wives, 100 Groupies and 27 Guitars*.

Clarissa winced. 'Even the order is wrong. At least start with guitars.'

'He wanted to start with groupies. Habit of a lifetime. At least he's paying me. Not like Steve Moran.'

'Not him again.' Clarissa raised her eyes heavenwards.

'The book's been out for a month. Could you please chase him up?'

'Perhaps you're taking on too much work. Get away. Mauritius, like Graham.'

'Clarissa, I can't afford to go to Mauritius! Or Margate, for that matter. Why do you think I take on so many projects? It's because I need the money from people like Steve Moran!'

'All right, I'll text him.'

'That's no good. He'll ignore that.'

'I could DM him?'

'I know it's old-fashioned, but could you please ring him?'

'Yes, of course, Nick. No need to get agitated.'

The door burst open. 'Oh, man! Sorry, you two, the Uber driver didn't know where he was going.' Junior Hamilton was six foot tall, all legs, with muscles in places Nick didn't even have places. He flaunted his physique by a close-fitting bottle green Armani suit, offset by matching tartan waistcoat and bow tie.

Clarissa's smile was dazzling. 'Oh, don't worry, Junior. These things happen.' She patted the chair next to her.

Junior threw his backpack on the floor and gave Clarissa an affectionate rub of the neck. 'Hey, Nick, what's going down?'

'Not much, actually.'

'That's where you're wrong, Nick. There is quite a lot going down.' Clarissa turned to face Junior. 'We've run into a bit of trouble. Legal trouble.'

'What kind?' Junior looked genuinely mystified. 'Every word is true. No lie.'

Clarissa studied her iPhone. 'Well, so far the publishers have been threatened with five libel suits, and they're getting pretty nervous. That's why they asked Graham — well, me — to see you. There are the two managers you called racist—'

'They were! One never picked me although I was in the England under-twenty-one team. And the other one was secretly in the British Movement.'

Clarissa linked her hands behind her back and leant back expectantly. 'Well, you didn't evidence either sufficiently. I'm afraid that's down to you, Nick.'

Nick shifted uneasily. 'It was libel-read!'

Clarissa consulted her notes. 'Then there's "Nobby" Smith, who you described as "aggressively and sexually narcissistic".'

Junior laughed. 'Did we put that? He wanked off in the shower so all the lads could see.'

Clarissa scrolled down. 'Your own ex-agent has accused you

of libel. Says he never demanded a holiday in the Caribbean for the West Bromwich Albion contract – whoever they are.'

'I did leave out that bent referee. *And* he's still reffing. Here, you should do him, Nick.'

The young receptionist strode in to hand Junior a latte.

'Thanks, darling.' He winked at her. 'Sweet.'

'Oh, it's my pleasure.' The receptionist had turned into the office vamp.

'Could I have—?' But she was out the door. Nick sagged back in his seat. 'Junior, you'll have to be careful what you say on *The One Show* tonight.'

'He'll be fine.' Clarissa looked admiringly at Junior. 'Just be yourself.'

'That's what I'm worried about,' muttered Nick.

'Make sure you talk about your foundation in the Caribbean.'

'It's just paying something back,' said Junior replied, expression saintly.

An appearance on *The One Show* was quite a coup, Nick thought. That should shift a few copies. But unfortunately no launch. Nick was of course disappointed – he always felt a book launch in some sprauncy venue was a vindication of his work, as well as a way of getting drunk at the publisher's expense. But he certainly wasn't going to fund it himself, as he had done on several occasions. He turned to Clarissa. 'So what are we going to do about all this?'

'Oh, the publishers will get another lawyer.'

Nick wasn't convinced. 'It's me that will need a lawyer, and I can't afford one.'

Clarissa smiled knowingly. 'You're such a worrier, Nick. You'll be protected by the agency. We have indemnity for this sort of thing.' She looked across at Junior, who rolled his eyes.

'He was like this when we were writing the book,' said Junior. 'Got into a right two-and-eight.'

Nick was about to recall all the missed meetings and broken promises, but decided against it. Then a thought occurred to him. 'If I've got nothing to worry about, what did you drag us down here for?'

Clarissa finally broke eye contact with Junior. 'To reassure you that, despite all the pending lawsuits, you've nothing to worry about.'

'Really?' Nick rubbed his face doubtfully.

'—I really needed to see Junior. We have some . . . loose ends to sort out over lunch. I've booked the usual spot, Junior.'

How come the author never got invited to these lunches? Nick got up to leave. 'Clarissa, please don't forget about Steve Moran. Oh, and Junior, you know you promised to get a signed Spurs shirt for the kid who lives upstairs.'

Backstage was a restaurant just off Leicester Square well known for its show business clientele. The lighting backlit the customer in a flattering way. The walls were festooned with memorabilia and signed photographs. Post-evening performance, the place was packed with performers, writers and other 'non-civilians'. Alan, the resident cocktail pianist, usually slightly inebriated, crouched, Bill Evans-style, over an upright in the corner, gently easing out show tunes and standards. He had been defeated for a request only once, when a diner asked him to play the show tune, 'You can see forever and forever more.'

Alan had insisted there was no such number until the diner accused him of being 'a phony', and the American actor Lee Hunter, then appearing at the Old Vic, had complained to the manager that the altercation was ruining his dinner. But he had then settled the argument by announcing that he had appeared in the musical *On a Clear Day* on Broadway, and this was the opening line of its signature tune. Alan was vindicated, but from then on he was wary of requests.

During the day the restaurant was much less busy, but still a haunt for those in the business. Kitty Lawrence was being helped into her seat at table 27 by her exasperated luncheon companion. 'Kitty, please God this one is all right.'

'I don't know why table three wasn't reserved for me as usual. I wasn't going to sit over there by the window and be gawped at. And I can't sit at the back, for reasons I won't go into. We know what we want,' said Kitty to the maître d' who'd been traipsing after them. 'And no, no aperitif, just a jug of water.'

Sam Goldman took his seat opposite her. Their sparring relationship had changed little since they had first met over 50 years ago at a first-night party. Neither had his attire of rust-coloured corduroys, black polo neck and London brogues – a look he had perfected in 1973 and found no reason to change. An instant and mutual dislike had, on a second meeting, become an acquaintance, and then a deep friendship. He had made a pass at her, of course, out of politeness, although he hadn't ever really found her alluring and had, until then, mainly enjoyed the company of men. He thought of himself as being bisexual, and found the current terminology of 'gender-fluid' both quaint and vulgar. In any case, Kitty had of course turned down his half-hearted advance, being primarily devoted and faithful to her husband, the saintly Ernest Forbes-Barrington. Rumours about a liaison with the RSC actor Edward Harcourt had nevertheless persisted among thespians for some years. Although occasionally tempted by Edward's matinee idol looks, Kitty had always denied any involvement – even to Sam.

'I don't think you've taken me out to lunch since I was at the Criterion.'

'I had to fight my way through your adoring fans.'

'And the first thing you said was, "You've done it again." I never quite knew what you meant.'

Sam laughed. 'Always sincere.'

'Mmm . . . But it is lovely to see you.' Kitty raised Sam's hand to her lips and kissed it.

'And while you're still alive.'

About ten years earlier Sam had been given a year to live. He'd sold his apartment in Nice and had anxiously got all his affairs in order. It later transpired that the medic had been overly pessimistic in his diagnosis, and Sam's heart condition had remained stable.

'It is extraordinary that I'm still here.'

'You should have sued your doctor, Sam. All that trouble you went to. To what do I owe the honour of this invitation, dear boy?'

'Well, apart from seeing you and catching up, I have a request.'

'Oh, not another charity thing, darling.'

'No, no. The thing is, I'd like—'

'Oh, I don't believe it. They've hung a portrait of Margaret Courtenay! Just because she got that gong. I suppose that's how you're rewarded for overacting.'

'I want you to write your autobiography.'

'Oh, Sam! Not again. You've been on at me about this for years.'

'Well, Maggie, Judi and Vanessa have all written theirs, and you've done better work than them.'

'You're only saying that because it's true.'

'It would be wonderful. You've had such a life. You've got so many marvellous stories.'

'Oh, I don't know. It'd be an awful lot of work.'

'Ah, well, that's where I can help. I have a very good ghost-writer friend. I've edited a few of his books over the years, and he's excellent.'

A nervous waiter appeared. 'What can I get for you, madame?'

'I'm starting with the avocado vinaigrette.' Kitty decided to be pre-emptive with her complaint. 'The last one I had here should have been called "Avocado concrete". Followed by the sole.' Kitty snapped her menu shut with a flourish and held it out at the waiter.

'And for you, sir?'

'I'll have the same. It will be a lot easier.'

'And to drink, madam?'

'We'll have a bottle of your house white. As long as it's dry.'

'No problem, madam.'

'I know it's not a problem. A problem would be if I forgot my lines or my agent dropped dead.' The waiter departed with a forced smile.

'The waiters here all used to be gay American dancers,' said Kitty. 'Now they're all Polish builder types.'

'As I was saying. Nick Greenwood, the ghostwriter, is very experienced.'

'He's not one of those who works from a shed at the bottom of his garden, is he? I'm too old to be dictating from a sit-on mower.'

'Don't be ridiculous.'

'Is he married?'

'Widowed.'

'Oh dear. How awful. When I lost Ernest, I couldn't eat or sleep for months. Not a bad bone in his body. Loved actors, even though he wasn't in the business.'

'Perhaps that's why.' Sam allowed himself a puckish smile. 'So, what do you say?'

Kitty was deep in thought. 'About what?'

'The book.'

'Oh, I'm really not sure.' The waiter arrived with the starters. Kitty stared at hers intently. 'I do hope that avocado is ripe.'

'At least meet Nick and see what you think. Look, there's a tea dance next week at the Royal Opera House. I could invite him.'

Kitty raised her voice dramatically. '*A tea dance*?' She picked up her spoon and attempted to attack her avocado. 'Oh! This is rock hard.'

*

Nick had been in therapy for about a year. He couldn't really afford it, but thought some objective counselling on the death of his wife and the effect on Ben, his career worries and general malaise might help. Initially he'd tried a directive counsellor, who turned out to have absolutely no sense of direction. Then he thought he'd be better off with a life coach – someone to guide his life and not explore his past – and found someone he thought might be helpful. 'You were born with wings,' blazoned her website. 'All you have to do is fly.' Nick discovered one of her clients had jumped off Beachy Head.

Then he decided he needed something more traditional, and entered the world of psychoanalysis. In the third session, when nothing had been said for 20 minutes, both Nick and his psychoanalyst had fallen asleep. The final therapist, Miriam, had accused him of falling in love with her, which she announced was quite usual due to the 'transference' between patient and therapist. This was clearly rubbish as Miriam was 75, obese and malodorous. When he told her he wasn't coming back she became tearful and exclaimed, 'How do you think that makes me feel?'

Nick was now seeing Deirdre, who described herself as a 'person-centred' therapist (who would want a therapist who was therapist-centred?), but he liked her. Deirdre was in her forties with a lovely lilting Dublin accent, intense green eyes and altogether very easy on the eye. Sensible and practical, she was analytical when necessary, and Nick enjoyed their fortnightly sessions. Indeed, he was probably becoming a little too dependent on her. She hadn't yet mentioned 'transference', but

Nick was hoping this might be a discussion for the future. Today, it was naturally the text from his GP that was really bothering him, but he had left it towards the end of the session.

Deirdre put down her notebook. 'So you rang the doctor?'

'Yes. Eventually.' Nick attempted what he thought was his most beguiling look.

'And what exactly did she say when she finally tracked you down?'

'She said they weren't happy with my blood results. Something showed up, and they were referring me to a specialist.'

'I see. What kind of specialist?'

'A urologist.'

'I see.'

'Deirdre, why do you keep saying "I see"?'

'There's nothing meant by it. Don't you go trying to interpret what I say, now. That's my job.'

'Well, it sounds like you know more than I do.'

'Of course I don't,' said Deirdre. 'So what are you thinking now?'

'The worst, of course.' Nick brushed imaginary dandruff from the shoulder of his Weird Fish fleece. 'You know me by now. I'm not exactly a glass-half-full person. I'm guessing what the problem is. Did you know, a man dies every forty-five minutes from prostate cancer?' Nick stared intently at Deirdre. 'I don't know how I'm going to tell Ben.'

'Do you need to tell him at this stage?'

'No. There's no point until I know more.'

'I expect you'll know when the time is right.' Deirdre smiled sympathetically and raised her hands in resignation. 'Talking of which, our time is up. We're going to have to end it for today.'

Nick was disappointed. They always seemed to be getting somewhere just when the session finished. 'Oh, OK. Thanks, Deirdre. I'll see you in a fortnight . . . if I'm still alive.'

3

Ben and Nick were tucking into fish and chips in front of the television, and had sat through a film about otters and a feature on sewers in the first ten minutes of *The One Show*. Ben was becoming restless. 'Dad, do we have to watch this?'

''Fraid so. Junior Hamilton is one of the guests. He's plugging our book. I mean his book. Our book.'

'How much of it did he actually write?'

'I don't think he's even bothered to read it. Be interesting to see what he says.'

'Marcel keeps asking me about the Spurs shirt.'

Nick forked a particularly stubborn chip. 'Don't worry. Junior will come through with it. Look, Junior's got a cousin with Down's syndrome. He understands.'

'When do you think, because—'

'For goodness' sake, Ben! I've told you. I'll sort it.'

'All right, Dad. All right.' Ben was taken aback. 'I was only asking.'

'I'm fine. Lot on my mind.'

'What's the matter? We're not broke, are we? Can't be that because we're always broke.'

'It's nothing. No need to worry.'

'I wasn't.'

'The GP said not to worry. So we mustn't.'

'The GP? Now I am worried.' Junior Hamilton appeared on screen. Ben grabbed the remote and pressed Pause. 'What's this all about?'

'Well.' Nick hesitated. 'I've been having a bit of trouble peeing.'

'And?'

'I've got to see a specialist. Just precautionary. But just in case, you ought to know. It's good to be prepared for the worst.' Nick was saying far more than he intended.

Ben was confused. 'The worst? But you didn't want to tell me. Make your mind up, Dad.' He looked at Nick long and hard. 'It can't be that serious. You look all right to me.'

'Thanks.'

'Can't lose you *and* Mum. That would make me an orphan.'

'I suppose it would.'

Ben smiled weakly. 'Still, everyone would be nice to me.'

Nick wondered where this discussion was going.

'I'll miss you of course, Dad.' Ben tapped his father on the knee affectionately. 'I mean, it would be great if you pulled through and everything. But you're right. I need to be prepared. Life must go on.'

'Well, yes. For some of us.'

Ben was warming to the conversation. 'I think we need to confront our fears. Be strong.'

'Must we?'

'I'll need to make plans.'

Nick felt Ben's stoicism was bordering on a suppressed eagerness to discuss his impending demise. 'Well, I'd try and go at a convenient time. I wouldn't want you to miss Glastonbury.'

'And you never know, there might be an upside to this.'

'Such as?'

'You won't have to worry about money any more. I can get in a lodger.'

'Look – *hang on*. I haven't even seen the specialist yet!'

'Do you think a tenant would pay more for your room? Then I wouldn't have to tidy my bedroom. In fact, I could let out all three rooms. Turn the whole flat into an Airbnb. Have that year in Thailand.'

Nick held his hands up in disappointment. 'You seem to be taking it all in your stride.'

'Be positive, you've always said.'

'Yes, but I haven't always meant it.'

'Marcel could have your laptop.'

The increasingly shabby set of *Southerners* was in turmoil. Landlord of the Queen's Head, Eddie Dunn, as portrayed by Steve Moran, was acting up rather than just acting. In the middle of local GP Maryam Kohli's dialogue he had flung down a pint glass which had shattered on the floor. 'Look, love, this isn't working.'

Shamina Shah, who played Dr Shams in the ever-popular television soap, was close to tears. 'I don't know what I'm doing wrong.'

'You're giving me nothing. It's like working with a mannequin.'

'I'm sorry, Steve. Perhaps it's the script.'

'The script doesn't help – why you would be trying to spill your heart about your gay son to me, of all people? But no, it's you, sweetheart, I'm afraid.' Steve paused. 'Again.'

'OK, folks.' The floor manager appeared and put an arm around the distraught actress. 'Never mind, Shamina. We can take five.' He began to clear up the broken pieces of sugar glass. Shamina sought refuge in the sympathetic arms of the make-up artist.

The soap's director, Alison Hess, put her head in her hands. She had worked on *Southerners* for three years, and had somehow survived the tantrums, demands and idiosyncrasies of a few 'difficult' actors and actresses, though any miscreant behaviour had been down to the need for perfection. But Steve Moran was in a league of his own.

The bullet-headed little Liverpudlian was universally unpopular for his scene-stealing antics and selfishness on set. Off set, to those who would listen –mostly new crew– he would talk behind the backs of other cast members, disparaging their performances and even their private lives with relish. Avoided by most of the cast at any social event, he saw himself as an international film star and above having to act in soaps. He had once knocked out a critic who had described him as a jobbing actor. He boasted of having been a semi-professional footballer, that he could have been a successful musician or indeed an artist. Whatever he did, he was always the best. He would have won both *Strictly Come Dancing* and *I'm A Celebrity . . . Get Me Out of Here* had he not been denied the chance to appear – something that was still a mystery to him and for which his agent bore the brunt of his ire. As penny-pinching as he was arrogant, Moran would never pay for even his own drinks. 'They can tell their chums they've bought Steve Moran a glass of wine.' He was married, surprisingly successfully, an arrangement which no-one could quite fathom.

Alison approached Moran. 'Look, we've done this scene five times.'

'Don't blame me. I told you it wasn't going to work. I gave you some re-writes.'

'In which Shamina hardly had a line.'

'Which is the best way, considering her lack of talent. Everyone knows she's useless.'

'Steve, Shamina is a well-regarded actress and very popular with the public. The suicide storyline brought in huge numbers of viewers.'

'That's because the punters were hoping she would jump off. It's about time I had a strong storyline. I'm fed up with all the domestic crap I get given.'

Steve was the third actor that week to have suggested a new storyline for their character. 'Fine', Alison reluctantly agreed. 'Let's discuss when we've wrapped up for the day, but can we please get this scene done.'

'Kev, I don't care how you do it. We need a fourth.' Charlie Robertson was getting desperate. 'Come on, you must know *someone.*' He put his mobile on speaker phone so that Bogdan Dimitrescu could hear the conversation.

'What about Leonard?'

His pal Kevin Styles laughed for longer than necessary. 'Still inside.'

'Oh.' Charlie was genuinely surprised.

'What about Del?' said Kev.

'You're joking! He's a fucking liability. That pyramid-selling scam nearly cost me a hundred grand. He always was giving it the old Barry McGuigan. I'll try Raymondo.' Charlie flung his mobile on the white leather sofa and turned to Bogdan. 'I don't know. Just can't get people these days.'

Bogdan, who was only slightly less imposing than an Exocet missile, shook his head. 'What you have planned, boss? Another bank job?'

Charlie bellowed with laughter. 'No, you berk. I'm playing in a charity event on Saturday. I need one more for my foursome. Here, you're handy with a club?'

'No golf courses in Romania. But Ceaușescu had one.'

'Is he any good?'

'Couldn't putt. Executed by firing squad.'

Charlie looked genuinely shocked.

'That's a bit harsh. Even by my standards.'

The village of Westlemere on the Suffolk coast had once been a thriving port, but many years of erosion had caused the demise of half of the village, and its harbour had long disappeared under the crashing waves of the North Sea. The fifteenth-century church had miraculously survived both the natural disaster and the Puritan assault in the guise of Thomas Cromwell's men, who had not only stripped the brass and stabled their horses in the vestry but also taken pot shots with their muskets at the carved angels in the roof. The pellet holes and the horse's hoofprints were still to be seen, and the highlight of Richard Greenwood's tour of the celebrated church (Saturday morning at 11, repeated at 2 p.m. during the summer.)

Another feature of the tour, and one which engrossed the 'customers', was the little-known tale of John and Robert Kennedy's brother Joseph P. Kennedy, a bomber pilot who had been killed in 1944 when his plane, a remote-controlled aircraft aimed at U-boats in the North Sea, exploded over the Suffolk countryside. The crew of two were supposed to bail out before the targets were hit, but tragically the Torpex bomb had gone off prematurely. Kennedy's remains were scattered in a nearby field, a catastrophe Richard took ghoulish delight in describing.

Richard Greenwood had been evacuated to Suffolk from the family home in Golders Green in the autumn of 1940. When he had stepped off the train at Ipswich, a doughty woman bearing an uncanny likeness to Joyce Grenfell had stepped forward and told the evacuation officer (who bore an uncanny likeness to Alastair Sim), 'I want him.'

'I'm afraid you can't, madam,' replied Richard's mother, who was one step behind. 'He belongs to me.' A three-way row ensued until it was verified that this was indeed Richard's mother and that of course they expected to be billeted together.

The two of them had ended up in a farmhouse in Westlemere, but this placement lasted only a month before Mrs Greenwood declared that she would rather risk Hitler's bombs than another night in the countryside. The peace and quiet of country life was unbearable, and she decided that bombs were less terrifying than WI meetings, beetle drives and village fetes. She missed the war-torn city too much. 'The bucolic life isn't for me,' she had declared. 'I like to hear the birds cough.' The mantra was repeated at every opportunity, long after she and Richard had returned to London.

But the village had left a mark on Richard and, following his retirement soon after the death of his wife, he had sought refuge in a small cottage overlooking the sea, precariously perched on the cliff edge. Richard immersed himself in village life, becoming a member and subsequently chair of the parish council, taking up the role of scorer for the cricket team and developing a love of birdwatching, becoming a leading light in the local twitchers' group.

The village now only numbered 300 residents, but he was fond of his neighbours. Lady Fitzherbert-Herbert, spinster of the parish and once a principal ballerina with the Royal Ballet, lived in the Priory, a fifteenth-century manor house reputed to maintain a secret tunnel to the church. Though she was now in her nineties, her annual talk to the WI about her escape from Dunkirk while touring with ENSA remained a key event, although audience numbers had dwindled with the passing years.

The local shop was run by the delightfully vague Ronnie Jellicoe, who had achieved this lifelong ambition after an unsatisfying career in the civil service. Unfortunately his knowledge of traffic systems far outweighed his skill in shopkeeping, and his stock of loofahs, pasta spoons and banana slicers was of little use to the villagers. He was also victimised by some of the children, who would ask for non-existent ice cream flavours and have him hunting in the freezer for their favourite bacon-and-egg ice lolly or double-pepperoni sorbet.

Richard shared a nightly pint at the Ship with Winston Butcher. When his wife of 45 years had passed away, the straight-talking farmworker, born and bred in the village, had pre-empted any possible pity by announcing to all the mourners at her funeral in a stentorian voice, 'Don't worry about me. I've gone and bought a microwave.' At the reception in the pub afterwards, Winston had handed out badges to all and sundry bearing the inscription 'Mustn't Grumble', and was later found sobbing in the gentleman's toilet.

This particular morning Richard had strayed several miles from Westlemere to do his shopping in the nearby market town of Blythwold. In the Co-op he spotted his intended target in the cold meat section. 'What a stroke of luck, I was hoping to bump into you.' Richard knew Cecil and Gladys Kett always did their shopping on Saturdays.

'Oh, good morning, Richard!' Cecil threw an out-of-date packet of honey roast ham on special offer into their trolley.

Gladys, slightly annoyed at being interrupted during her weekly shop, managed a brusque 'Hello.'

'Excellent.' There was a momentary awkward silence before Richard went on. 'I saw your piece in the *Gazette*.'

'Oh.' Cecil looked pleased. 'Amazing, isn't it?' Gladys didn't appear quite so delighted.

'Who'd have thought?' Cecil was delighted that Richard seemed genuinely enthralled.

'Yes, who'd have thought?' Gladys raised her eyes heavenwards.

The article to which the two men were referring featured an interview with Cecil, who had recently discovered that his father, whom he'd never known, was a United States Air Force serviceman of Native American descent. Even more extraordinarily, Cecil, a squat, hirsute, 60-year-old unemployed welder with strong features and eyebrows you could stuff cushions with, had recently been contacted out of the blue by his half-sister, a representative of the Golden Eagle tribe, and advised that he was actually a tribal chief, entitled to a home and a number of acres of reservation land in New Mexico. According to the article, Cecil was planning to travel to the 'Land of Enchantment' for the initiation ceremony and take up his position after Easter.

'I've never heard such a thing,' said Richard. 'It's going to change your life.'

'Both our lives. I don't want to go. I'm a Suffolk girl. I don't want to be an Indian squaw.'

'"Native American", Glad. I keep telling you. In any case, you'll still be Mrs Kett, not a squaw.'

'Is that meant to make me feel better?' Gladys turned to Richard for support. 'Ever since he found out about this, he's been impossible. He just watches Westerns all the time.'

Cecil nodded enthusiastically. 'Have you ever seen *Broken Arrow*, Richard? I see myself as a sort of Jeff Chandler. I reckon I've got that rugged nobility he achieved when he played Cochise.'

Gladys snorted. 'Well, he wasn't even an Indian.'

'"Native American". Gladys, you've got to start treating my ancestors with respect.'

'I came home the other day and found him dressed from head to toe in feathers, headdress, buckskin and war paint.'

'The paper wanted a picture.'

'They put it on the front page. You looked ridiculous.'

'You know what, Richard, I can claim a ceremonial name.'

Gladys sniggered. 'What's it going to be? Big Chief Sitting About?'

'They are even giving me a special pow-wow.'

Richard felt it time to intervene. 'It's a wonderful story, Cecil. Have you . . . ever thought about a book?'

'Oh, I'm not one for publicity. I always tick that box when I buy a lottery ticket. Not that I ever win anything. Story of my life up until now.'

'You wouldn't know where to start,' said Gladys. 'I think we could do with some chicken thighs.'

'This is what my son does, Cecil. He helps people write their memoirs.'

'Well, I've done a lot of reading about my people,' Cecil pronounced proudly.

'That's a good start.'

'Do you know, Richard, the white man made many promises,

but he kept only one. They said they were going to take our land, and they took it.'

'I thought that was the National Trust,' muttered Gladys.

'Your story deserves to be told, Cecil,' said Richard.

As Richard bade farewell to the Ketts and pushed his trolley towards the ready meals section, he thought it prudent not to point out that life on a modern reservation was a long way from the romantic idyll Cecil was hoping for. A depressing picture of alcoholism, lawlessness and gambling, in fact. A bit like Lowestoft.

On his way home Richard left a voice message for Nick. 'You'll be glad to know I've got you another job. Ring me when you can.'

The remains of a heavy frost glistened on the brass plaques as Nick made his way around the extensive rose garden of the local crematorium, deep in thought. He felt a tap on his shoulder, and turned to see his neighbour Grace King, wrapped up against the cold in a long grey woollen trench coat. A black Russian-style fleece hat and matching scarf pulled tight under her chin framed Grace's striking features. She was, he had to admit, extremely easy on the eye.

'Hello, Grace. What are you doing here? Sorry, silly question.'

'Visiting my aunt. You?'

'Same as you. Well, I'm not visiting your aunt.' The two of them laughed uneasily.

'My wife. She's in the rose garden. I mean, her ashes are. I thought a wall tablet or a leather panel a little ostentatious.'

'Ha. My aunt demanded a place in the garden vault. She was like that.'

They both laughed again.

'Oh dear,' said Grace. 'We're not exactly intruding on each other's grief, are we?'

'Amy died last year. I like to visit her occasionally. Of course, she shouldn't really be here. She was American.'

'Don't they allow Americans to be here?'

Nick smiled. 'Her family wanted her shipped back to LA, but Ben and I wanted her here. We won.'

'You've never talked much about her.'

'No. It's all a bit complicated. We had what you might say was a difficult relationship. I thought we were rubbing along quite nicely until I discovered she was having an affair. I was watching *Escape to the Country*, and while Alastair Appleton was wittering on I saw her walking into a hotel with another man. It was a repeat, too.'

'Oh,' was all Grace could come out with.

'Anyway, she decided to set up home with him, and so we separated. Turned out her lover was a right prick. Total control freak. She wanted to come back, but I said no. And three years ago she became ill.'

'What about her partner?'

'Oh, he scarpered when Amy had the stroke.'

Grace struggled momentarily for a response. 'And what about Ben? How did he cope with it all?'

'Not very well. He was only eleven when Amy deserted us. We've never really talked about it.'

'Did you visit Amy in hospital?'

'Once or twice. I don't think she knew I was there. It was just awful. Despite what happened, I couldn't bear to see her like that.'

'What about Ben?'

'Never. It was ten years ago that she ran off and he never forgave her. I tried to encourage him, said it was important when she did pass away. And then what with Covid he wasn't allowed to visit.'

Grace shook her head. 'I'm so sorry for him,' she sighed. 'Ben's a lovely boy. He's great with Marcel.'

'Well, he's very fond of Marcel. Like a little brother.'

'Did you not want more children?'

'Oh, yes. People used to ask us why we only had one child. We tried for years to conceive, and didn't think we could have any. We were in the process of adopting when she became pregnant with Ben.'

'And you stopped the adoption?'

'The adoption agency told us we had to. And we had been desperate to adopt. We'd been through hell. They described it as "a journey".'

Nick and Amy had gone to incredible lengths to convince the adoption agency that they could provide the cultural background for an American child to be adopted – their best bet at the time. Other couples in the preparation group had advised them that the agencies were very keen on that sort of thing, and so, before the social worker came round, a 'Stars and Stripes' flag was hung in the driveway, copies of Steinbeck novels were strewn across the coffee table, set against the background strains of Bruce Springsteen. Amy even baked a cherry pie.

'But you must have both been thrilled when Amy became pregnant?'

'Of course. Seemed like a miracle. Maybe the pressure was off when we decided to adopt. Amy had thought it would never happen.' Nick fell silent.

'People still ask me why I had Marcel.'

'Really?'

'Absolutely. And if I knew that I was having a baby with Down's syndrome.' By the expression on Nick's face Grace could see that he wanted to know the answer, and rescued him. 'Yes, I did know.'

Grace thought back to the time when it was confirmed by a scan and blood test that Marcel had Down's syndrome. Initially, she had been in complete shock. This wasn't meant to happen. Her partner had been insistent that they shouldn't keep the baby, and that having a disabled child would ruin their relationship. Grace would need to choose between the baby and him. As far as he was concerned she would have to have a termination: it was cruel, he said, bringing 'someone like that' into the world. It struck Grace that she didn't want to be with 'someone like that.' So she threw him out.

Initially after the birth she struggled, and even with the support of her family wondered how she would cope in the years ahead. She was distraught that she didn't bond with Marcel immediately, and for the first weeks mourned the loss of the child she *had* been expecting. It was only when Marcel became a character in his own right – Marcel who had Down's syndrome; not a baby with Down's syndrome who was called

Marcel. And it was Marcel's first smile that really captured her heart.

'I haven't asked you about your aunt.'

Grace shrugged. 'Don't worry. She was a battleaxe. I do this for my mother, her sister. Strange how our parents can still control the way we live after they've passed.'

'And not just our parents.' Nick stared at Grace. 'You look cold.' He put his arm around her, and quickly removed it. 'Sorry.'

'That's OK. It is freezing. I'd better get back to work.' Grace hesitated momentarily. 'Listen, I have a huge favour to ask. Can I pop in and see you sometime?'

'Sure. Tell me now.'

'Well, it actually involves Ben too. I need to talk to both of you.'

'Oh.' Nick was intrigued, even though he had a date with an octogenarian and he was running late.

Nick and Grace exited the crematorium in reflective silence. Nick hoped Grace didn't mind the fleeting physical contact, and had actually surprised himself with this protective gesture. He had never had this sort of intimate conversation with his upstairs neighbour. Strange that they should do so in such bleak surroundings. Perhaps it was their shared experience of loss that had allowed him to open up to her. Who was it had written, 'Death lays bare the bones of truth'?

4

The spacious and elegant Paul Hamlyn Hall on the ground floor of the Royal Opera House was already thronged for the Friday afternoon tea dance. Extra male dancers had been enlisted so that single women of advancing years would not feel left out. A small orchestra played in front of the huge iron-and-glass dome. Sam and Kitty, in the midst of a good many other older couples, waltzed slowly around the hall, Sam expertly steering the fragile Kitty around the floor. Kitty closed her eyes and imagined she was dancing with husband Ernest in a world that had long passed.

Nick stood at the edge of the highly polished dance floor trying to catch Sam's eye. Sam ignored him until the strains of *The Blue Danube* ended, and he and Kitty turned to applaud the musicians before making their way over to a table. He gestured to Nick to join them. 'Kitty, I'd like to introduce you to my good friend Nick Greenwood.'

'Hi Kitty, pleased to meet you.' Nick bent down to kiss the actress's cheek.

Kitty didn't approve of the kiss, and even less of the 'Hi'. 'Good afternoon.' Looking the writer up and down, she also felt he was somewhat shoddily dressed for this meeting. Nick Greenwood was already somewhat of a disappointment to her. 'Delighted to meet you.'

Nick smiled. 'That was a very graceful waltz, Kitty.'

'Thank you.'

'And, Sam, I hadn't realised you were quite so elegant on the dance floor. Quite the Fred Astaire.'

Kitty brightened. 'I met him once. Charming. But a taskmaster when it came to work, I believe.'

'Kitty has some wonderful stories of old Hollywood.' Sam looked expectantly across the table.

Nick was immediately interested. 'Oh, really?'

'Ghastly place. Well, I did make several "pictures", as they like to call them. Sam, dear, I must visit the Ladies.' The two men rose to help Kitty to her feet, but she waved them away. 'There's really no need,' she snapped. 'As you have both witnessed, I'm not a cripple.'

'You should have dressed up,' muttered Sam when Kitty was gone.

'I'm wearing a tie!'

'But jeans – *honestly*. It's not a rodeo. And trainers! What's the matter with you?'

'OK, OK. She's rather grand, isn't she?'

'Well, yes. Compared to you, dear boy. She's just old school. You'll get used to her.'

'Has she got any money?'

Sam glared at Nick. 'Now that is vulgar. Yes, a great deal. Her late husband was a High Court judge.'

'Good, because I'll need a decent fee for once – and one that gets paid. And I suppose you'll want a percentage for the introduction.'

'Don't be ridiculous, Nick. I'm doing you both a favour.'

On Kitty's return both men rose to their feet. 'Would you like some tea, Kitty?'

'Yes, please, Sammy, dear. You be mother.'

Kitty turned her nose up at the Digestive biscuits, declaring they looked stale.

Nick swiftly moved onto the real reason they were there. 'Well, Kitty – sorry, Miss Lawrence – have you thought of writing an autobiography?'

'It had never crossed my mind until Sam mentioned it last week.'

'That's where I come in, Miss Lawrence. I can guide you and help with the writing. But it would be your book. You'd have the final say.'

'Well, of course. Who else? I'd have to get to know you before I could come to trust you.'

Sam nodded enthusiastically. 'That's one of the most important aspects of the relationship, isn't it, Nick?'

'There would be some things that are not for public consumption,' continued Kitty.

Nick didn't exactly put Kitty down as a kiss-and-tell merchant, but had been hoping he might coax some theatrical secrets out of her. 'I understand,' he replied, disingenuously.

Kitty sighed dramatically. 'I feel I have something still to give my public. Even at my age. It's terrible when you are so old that people look at you and think you'd be better off dead.'

'People have looked at me like that most of my life,' Nick said, more loudly than he intended.

'I'll need time to collect my thoughts.'

'Of course, but it would be best to start as soon as possible.'

'I'm not about to keel over and die, Mr Greenwood.'

'I think he means he's very excited by the idea,' said Sam.

'Oh, I am,' Nick replied uncertainly.

They strolled out onto Bow Street towards Covent Garden underground station, with Kitty on Sam's arm and Nick on the other side in a kind of protective formation. At the Tube Kitty released herself from the two men and announced she would mull the idea over. Sam grasped Kitty's hands. 'Trust me, Kitty, he's a very dependable chap. With Nick, what you see is what you get.'

A black SUV with tinted windows screeched to a stop beside them. A burly, shaven-headed man in chinos and a puffa jacket jumped out, uttered 'Excuse me, ma'am', and threw Nick into the back, banging his head on the door frame, before jumping in after him. The car revved loudly and sped off.

Kitty and Sam stared after it as it weaved in and out of the traffic. Kitty was the first to recover. 'Good gracious. Should we do anything?'

Sam affected unconcern. 'He must have ordered a taxi without telling us.'

Kitty eyed Sam with suspicion. 'I've never seen such an enthusiastic cabbie.'

'Those Uber chaps can be a bit brusque, I've heard.' Sam motioned for Kitty to retake his arm.

*

Slumped next to Bogdan Dimitrescu in the back seat of the SUV, Nick was clutching his head. 'You bastards! You could have fractured my skull — you know that?'

The driver sniggered. 'Take more than that, bro.' Leon Brathwaite was a former heavyweight boxer and bouncer. 'I know. I've done that a couple of times.'

Nick recovered himself. 'Every sodding time. You're meant to do the hand-on-the-head thing. Like they do on the television. I thought you used to be a policeman, Bogdan?'

Leon glanced in the rear-view mirror. 'He was, like, a secret policeman, wasn't you? Don't think they done that in the Stasi.'

Bogdan looked contemptuously at Leon. 'I spit on the Stasi.'

'Sorry, mate. KGB, was it?'

'Securitii Stalului. Romania. We scare fuck out of KGB. KGB were pussies.' Bogdan, lost in reverie, was looking out of the window. 'Securitate was most feared. In whole world.'

Leon looked serious. 'You've never met a Millwall supporter, have you, Bog?'

Nick was bent over with his head in his hands. 'You could at least be more careful.'

'Where I come from, careful is not so important. Why should I take care? Two hours later body be floating face down in Dambovita river.'

Leon brightened. 'Don't you worry, Mr Greenwood. He's talking about the good old days.'

Bogdan chuckled. 'I kill no-one since last Monday.'

Somewhere in the wilds of Ongar, Essex, the car carrying the three men pulled up outside a security gate bearing the name 'Tu

Lions' in large lead letters. Punching in a code, which silently opened the doors, Leon drove up the gravel carriage drive passing a multitude of security lights and warnings about guard dogs. He brought the car to a halt with a satisfying crunching sound. The two heavies began to haul Nick out.

'I can manage this bit, thank you.' He shrugged off their grip to stand facing the impressive building, a white, weather-boarded period property with red tiled roof and porch, spectacular bay windows and a single goalpost occupying the front garden. 'What does he want this time?'

Bogdan shrugged, 'He is law until himself.'

'The gaffer likes to unburden himself.' Leon patted Nick on the back comfortingly. 'He sees you as a sort of therapist.'

'Nick, my old mucker.' Charlie Robertson was crunching across the gravel. Charlie was a rangy figure, dressed in a bottle-green velour tracksuit over a black-and-white Jack Daniel's T-shirt. His salt-and-pepper hair was slicked back, framing a craggy face that could only be described as 'lived in'. His aquiline nose was surprising considering what it had been subjected to over the years. 'Glad you could make it.'

Nick massaged his still aching neck. 'Didn't seem I had much choice.'

Charlie put his arm around Nick and guided him through the studded solid oak front door, which was framed by two enormous crouching stone lions. Despite his advancing years Charlie was still in good shape, and very little of his hard-earned muscle had turned to fat.

Nick had taken over the writing of Charlie's autobiography,

Innocent – On My Childrens' Eyes, a year previously when his then collaborator, an investigative journalist, Phil 'Nosey' Parker, had mysteriously disappeared halfway through the project. Nick had asked Charlie several times what had happened to him, but was particularly discommoded by Charlie's chuckle at the word 'ghost.'

But the writing of *Innocent* had gone surprisingly smoothly. Charlie had always stuck to his deadlines, and Nick had always been transported to their meetings punctually, albeit clumsily, by Leon or Bogdan.

Charlie led Nick into his games room and indicated the full-sized snooker table. 'Pour yourself a drink. Fancy a game while we talk?' He arched a cue javelin-style in Nick's direction, which Nick dropped.

Nick retrieved the cue and helped himself to a large single malt from the decanters and cut-glass tumblers on the sideboard.

Charlie crouched over the table and sent the red balls to all quarters of the green baize. One dropped into a middle pocket. 'Lucky break.'

'You can always ring me. Is this gangster thing really necessary?'

'Just my style, Nick. It guarantees your company.'

'Are we talking about a second volume?'

Charlie snorted. 'Not likely.'

'Want to repent?'

'You know I've made my peace with the Lord.'

'I was pleased with that chapter,' said Nick.

'What, all that born-again stuff? Finding the Lord in prison? I made it up.'

Nick's mouth fell open. 'You what?'

'You got a chapter out of it. Being a bit of a Bible-basher is expected from someone like me.' Charlie potted the pink and positioned himself for his next shot. 'I've got a little problem I'd like you to help me with. I don't want anyone else to know until you've made some initial findings.'

'I'm not a private detective.'

'They are fucking useless, 'scuse my lingo.' Charlie missed his next red, recorded his total on the mahogany-and-brass scoreboard. 'There, I've left you a lot on.' Nick took another slug of Laphroaig and lined up the white ball. 'And, most importantly I trust you.' Nick's host clapped him on the back. 'It's Ashley. My youngest. She disappears all day and some evenings. Don't know what she gets up to and she refuses to tell me. She's usually back around ten o'clock, so I'm not too worried. More curious.'

'How old is she?' Nick had forgotten the names and ages of Charlie's various offspring.

'Twenty-two. Doesn't seem possible.'

'Well, she's old enough to lead her own life.'

'Don't be a wally. She'll always be my baby.'

'It's really not my thing. And besides which I haven't been feeling that well recently. Waterworks trouble. I've actually got a hospital appointment soon.'

'You want to get that sorted, Nick. Nip it in the bud.'

'Bugger!' Nick had screwed up an easy red.

'Have another go.'

Nick miscued and sent the black spinning into one of the side pockets. 'Oh dear. I am rubbish.'

'Let's give this a miss. Come on, sit down. Like I was saying, you don't want to leave it till it's too late. Otherwise you'll end with a rubber tube up your todger. My mate Kev told me he squealed like a pig when he had it done.' Charlie made a chopping motion. 'And he'd enjoyed a session with Mad Frankie Fraser.'

Nick studied his glass and drained the contents. Charlie refilled their tumblers and led him into a sitting room the size of Chigwell. Pointing him to a white leather sofa he handed him a gilt photo frame. The picture showed Charlie in dress suit with his arm around a beautiful but bored-looking brunette. Her expression revealed even more than her dress. Charlie shook his head with pride. 'That's us at Ascot last year. Private box in the Royal enclosure. Had four winners. One of the best days of my life. Up there with hearing Desmond Squirrel had jumped off London Bridge. Beautiful, isn't she?'

'Yes, yes, she is.'

Nick had interviewed three of Charlie's grown-up children, but had never met Ashley. He certainly would have remembered. 'What do you want me to do?'

'Follow her. See what she's up to and report back.'

Nick swallowed the rest of his whisky. 'Charlie, I've never done this sort of thing. Why can't you get Leon or Bogdan to follow her? Surely that's the sort of thing you employ them for?'

'She knows them too well. I want to keep this private.'

'Look, Charlie, in this job I'm often used as a PA, an odd-job man, even a shrink. But never a gumshoe. Haven't you got anyone else?'

'Yeah. But they're all villains. I don't want the whole of my manor to know. How does five grand sound?'

Nick took another gulp of malt. 'That is generous, Charlie. I could do with the money . . .' A thought hit him. 'You didn't ask my predecessor to do this sort of thing, did you?'

Charlie shook his head. 'Complete berk.'

'What did happen to him, Charlie?' Before Nick could press Charlie further, his mobile vibrated. Nick checked the caller ID. Frankie Morrison. 'Do you mind if I get this?'

'Go ahead. I'll get us some more drinks.'

'I spoke to Harvey,' said Frankie. 'We agreed to meet. Took a lot of balls to ring him, I can tell you.'

Nick was genuinely surprised. He had been urging Frankie without success to let him talk to Aslan's Roar's drummer. Once best mates, Frankie and Harvey Love had fallen out over the royalties to the band's hit single 'Narnia Groove' in 1971 and hadn't spoken since.

'Terrific. You want me to come along?'

'Bit delicate. He's also never forgiven me for stealing his chick – you know?'

Nick didn't. 'OK, great. Let me know how it goes.'

Charlie returned with both tumblers filled to the brim. 'So, what d'you say, Nick?'

Nick took a large swig. The blow on the head and the copious amounts of single malt had left him a little befuddled. 'Well . . .'

'Go on. Spit it out.'

Nick paused. 'There is something that has been bothering me.'

'What's that?'

'Well, there's a bloke that owes me money. It's gone on a long time. And—'

'What's his name?'

'Steve Moran. A so-called soap star.'

'Never heard of him. How much?'

'Ten grand. I know it's not much to you, Charlie, but—'

'It's the principle. I've always had principles, as you know. Tell you what. If I get you the money we call it quits on your fee for finding Ashley.'

'But please don't take it too far, will you, Charlie? I don't want any trouble.'

Charlie nodded sagely. 'Consider it sorted. Now, finish your drink. You don't play golf, do you? I'm looking for a fourth.'

'Golf, no. I'm even worse at golf than I am at snooker.'

Charlie looked unsurprised. 'Don't ever go to Romania. They are fucking strict with bad golfers.'

Frankie gave Nick a thumbs-up and mouthed, 'Hello, Nick.'

'Frankie, I can't hear you. Unmute.'

The muso shook his head and pointed to his ears. Nick had thought an online session might save him some time, but he was beginning to regret his suggestion. 'You need to unmute the volume on your laptop.'

Frankie had struggled to sign into his Zoom meeting, and now his girlfriend, Lucy, who had helped him, had disappeared.

'Turn up your sound settings.'

Frankie shrugged.

'The mic icon, Frankie. Bottom left-hand corner.'

Frankie made a show of searching before raising his left hand helplessly.

'It's a *microphone*, Frankie,' Nick muttered to himself. 'You've seen one of those.'

Frankie's eyes lit up as he discovered and clicked on the icon. 'Here we go.'

'*Finally*. I thought musicians were meant to be technical.'

'I'm all right with an amp. Never got round to producing.'

'Frankie, I can only see the top of your head. You just need to' – Nick's screen went blank – 'move the laptop.'

'Better?'

'Now I can hear you, but I can't see you.'

'Video button. Thought that might help.'

'No, it didn't. Click on it again. Can't you get Lucy back in?' Lucy seemed to be quite a good influence on Frankie, and Nick had considered talking to her, but she and Frankie had only been together for a few months and, since she was about 30 years younger, Nick wasn't convinced the relationship would last.

'She's cooking. Here, is this working?' Frankie's face returned to view.

'Yes, well done, Frankie. Now don't touch anything. We've only got an hour. Well ... less now. And I've got a medical appointment straight after this.'

'Sorry to hear that, man. Did I tell you about my hernia?'

'No. Listen, I've been trying to get hold of your old band members for about a fortnight.'

'Sticking out from my guts like a cantaloupe melon.'

'What?'

'My hernia.'

'They won't talk to me unless you give them the OK.'

'I'd go private if I had the money. There's a fucking long waiting list at my local hospital. It's those health tourists, I reckon.'

This wasn't the time to lecture Frankie on NHS cuts and *Daily Mail* headlines, so Nick avoided continuing the discussion. 'You also said you would give me your mum's contact details.'

'Did I? Poor old Mum died years ago. Not a day goes by when I don't want to talk to her.'

'But I thought—?'

'Knocked down by a bus.'

Another valuable resource for the book had been lost.

'Stepped in front of it on her way to work. Driver was drunk. Mind you, so was she.'

'Do you have any other aunts or uncles who might be able to help?'

'I suppose you could try talking to my sister.'

'You have a *sister*?'

'Yeah. Ella. Named after Ella Fitzgerald. My dad loved her. Ella Fitzgerald, that is. My sister not so much.'

Nick slumped in his chair. He had been 'working' with Frankie for over a year, and this was the first time he had mentioned a sister. He could hear Frankie's name being called. Frankie turned his head away and shouted, 'OK, babe. Coming.'

He returned to the screen. 'Sorry, Nick, grub's up. She gets pissed off if I'm late.'

A message on Nick's screen revealed that Frankie was leaving the meeting.

'Mr Greenwood?' There was a spring in the step and a dazzling smile on the face of the Filipino urology nurse as Nick followed her silently down the corridor. 'Isn't it a lovely day?'

Nick thought the day was anything but lovely, having already waited half an hour trying not to imagine that the other patients around him were all in the final stages of their illness. Was this part of an NHS initiative to relax patents before delivering some terrible hammer blow? Or maybe the results were good and she was conveying them to him sub-textually without breaking any guidelines. Or maybe she was just a happy soul who loved her work. Nick's head was spinning.

'Oh, that's a perfect weight for your height,' beamed the nurse. What did she mean by 'perfect'? By the time she took his blood pressure Nick was in something of a restrained frenzy.

'Mmm, I think we'll do that again,' she chortled, pumping the cuff on his arm. 'That's better.'

'Am I the best patient today?' Nick tried weakly to match the nurse's good mood.

'Ha! Nice one,' she replied, barely containing her hilarity.

The consultant, on the other hand was hatchet-faced. The gloomy way in which the twin-suited and smartly coiffured Dr Hanson gestured him to sit down was clearly a sign of things to come. She might as well be consigning him to the electric chair. Her opening gambit of 'How are you feeling?' was filled with double-edged nuance. What on earth did she mean by that?

'Fine, thanks,' Nick mumbled.

'I'm sorry, I'm running late, so I need to be quick.' Dr Hanson gave Nick what he construed as a death stare. 'Well, I wouldn't say the results were disastrous, but the bloods showed that your PSA was quite high for a man of your age.'

'Oh.'

'PSA measures the prostate specific antigen in your blood, and gives us a clue to your condition.'

'How high was mine?'

'Twenty-six.'

'What is it meant to be?'

'Somewhere between nought and four.'

'Ah.' Nick didn't really know what that meant either, but it didn't sound good. That duplicitous nurse. He'd have a word with her on the way out.

'It could be caused by an enlarged prostate,' Dr Hanson continued, 'due to other factors, but can be an indication of prostate cancer. So we need to perform a biopsy.'

Nick's look of panic brought a reassuring look from Dr Hanson. 'Don't worry, it's a very common procedure. Day surgery. And once we have the results, we can decide on the treatment. In the meantime there's not much more we can do. Keep as active as possible. What do you do for a living?'

'I'm a writer.'

'Ah ... so you probably spend a lot of time hunched over a computer. And at night – how is your flow?'

'Not sure about at night' – Nick attempted a little levity – 'but I try to manage a thousand words a day.'

Dr Hanson gave a fleeting smile. 'The flow of *urine*.'

'Sorry. Not too bad. I have to get up once or twice.'

Dr Hanson was already on her feet and offering him a farewell handshake. 'And if it is the worst scenario, prostate cancer is the most common form of the disease in men, and you can live with it for years.'

'I'd rather live without it.'

'You'll probably die with it, not because of it.'

'Any idea when? I've got several books to finish.'

Dr Hanson laughed the laugh of Medea. 'Oh, we don't want to get into prognosis at this stage. One step at a time. Anything else you'd like to ask?'

Nick had heard enough. 'No, that's OK, thanks.'

Nick passed the Filipino 'angel' on his way out. She was laughing even more uproariously as she weighed another patient. Poor devil, Nick thought. He'll only have a couple of weeks to live.

Across town, the creative staff of *Southerners* were finalising the departure of Steve Moran's character, Eddie Dunn. His mental and subsequent physical abuse of Shamina had led to suspension and an immediate executive decision to dismiss Moran from the show, much to the relief of everyone. Storylines were re-written with glee in order to end Moran's days on the soap. It would need to be a dramatic send-off.

'He's got to die.' The chief writer, Julia Browne, was

adamant. 'We don't want him to just disappear and come back some time.'

'Violently,' added the producer, Alison Hess.

'Suicide?'

'That might elicit some sympathy.'

'Maybe at the hands of Shamina?'

'Nice, but we don't want her character implicated. Could be a health-and-safety accident?'

'He's a postman.'

'Torn to pieces by a customer's XL bully!'

The discussion continued for a couple more hours in mounting hysteria until a fitting end for Steve Moran was agreed on. The creatives agreed it was the most enjoyable writing session since the immolation of the universally despised Terry Fletcher.

The task of informing Moran was left to the series head. Surprisingly, he took the news remarkably well. 'I was planning to leave anyway,' he told his fellow cast members. 'I've had lots of offers recently, and *Southerners* is just holding me back. In fact, I feel sorry for you all. You'll be stuck here for the rest of your lives.'

His thoughts inevitably dominated by Dr Hanson's gloomy proclamations, Nick had considered cancelling his appointment with Kitty Lawrence in favour of the pub, or anywhere that provided some comfort. He had decided, however, that work might be a welcome distraction. He rang the glistening brass bell at the actress's handsome, whitewashed Georgian house in

Teddington, and the door was opened by Kitty's housekeeper clasping a feather duster.

'Oh. The writer. Wipe your feet properly.' Nick performed an elaborately choreographed routine on the doormat. 'All right, no need to make a song and dance about it.' The cleaner led him into a stately drawing room dominated by a grand crystal chandelier, an enormous gilt-framed mirror, an Italian walnut armoire, a bamboo cocktail bar with a black Formica top and a collection of oil paintings, mainly of Kitty. Fluorescent red-and-gold-striped curtains bound by gold rope completed the faded grandeur. William Morris said you should have nothing in your house you don't know to be useful or beautiful. He must have been visiting Kitty Lawrence's abode. Photographs of a distinguished-looking man at various stages of his life, but always be-suited, were dotted around the room.

'And before you begin' – the housekeeper was glaring at him – 'we don't want any scurrilous stuff written about Miss Lawrence.'

'Oh, that's not my style.' Nick hoped she had never read his book *Screw Them All*, about an infamous film director turned restaurant critic.

Kitty was propped up on a velvet-covered armchair, framed by French windows, beyond which a perfect lawn led to the Thames.

'Good afternoon, Miss Lawrence. What a wonderful place you have here.'

'Thank you. Ernest and I bought the house in 1973. It holds many happy memories.' Kitty dismissed her cleaner with an imperious wave. 'Now, Mr Greenwood, I have a few questions before I commit myself to this autobiography. How is this going to work?' There was an air of menace in Kitty's voice.

'Mainly through interviews, which I'll record. I'll make some notes and talk to your friends and family.'

'I have no family. But despite my age, I still have plenty of close friends. I have also kept journals since 1963 – will that help?'

'Just what we ghostwriters love to hear.'

'They're stuffed full of theatrical anecdotes.'

'May I borrow them?'

'As long as you look after them properly.' Kitty regarded Nick intensely over her half-moon glasses.

'Of course. It's most important that I have your trust.'

'The last time I trusted anyone I didn't know that well was an actress who made a pass at Ernest. It was the opening night party for *Arms and the Man*. She was never heard of again. I made sure of it.'

Nick blinked. 'Should I be writing this down?'

'No need. I've made some notes in these exercise books. My journals. And I expect you'll want to see some photographs,' Kitty went on. 'I've looked out a few for you' – and she handed him a frayed leather album. Nick flicked through a number of images of Kitty in various theatrical productions and some family snaps, which would be very useful for the book.

'Can I borrow this, Kitty?'

'This is even more precious.'

'I'll guard it with my life.' Nick held the album close to his chest. 'I promise.'

'Do you have a publisher in mind?'

'Don't worry, I'll sort that out.'

'And you'll need a fee.'

'Yes, Kitty.' This was the bit Nick hated. 'We should settle on a figure before we get started, and then I'll draw up a contract between us.'

'Well, I've spoken to Sam, and he's suggested a reasonable amount.'

Nick had been planning to ask £15,000 – worth a try – but after some negotiation, at which Kitty was much more adept, a sum of £10,000 was agreed. Five up front and five on delivery. Still, it seemed like an assignment he'd rather enjoy.

On his way out Nick touched the housekeeper gently on the shoulder and dispensed his most charming smile. 'Oh – Edie. I'd very much like to interview you . . . I'm sure you can give me some delightful insights into how lovely it must be to work for Miss Lawrence.' Edie's lips broke into a half-smile. 'Your contribution might prove invaluable.' And having concluded his John Le Mesurier impersonation, Nick departed.

On the way home, he rang Sam.

'Hello, dear boy. Well, I think you've cleared the first fence. In fact, she seemed rather impressed.'

'It would have been even better if you hadn't suggested a fee.'

'You weren't going to try and bilk the old girl?'

'You said she was wealthy and—'

'Listen, dear heart, you're lucky to get any fee these days. I wanted to ask you – who on earth were those goons who picked you up outside the Opera House the other day?'

'Friends of a friend. You remember me telling you about Charlie Robertson?'

'I thought you were a goner. Presumed you'd be found in tiny pieces, sprinkled on a desolate farm on Dartmoor.'

'You didn't do much to help.'

'Kitty waved her stick at them as you sped away. I think she rather enjoyed it. Probably got you the job.'

'Anyway, Charlie has something he wants me to do for him, and in return I asked him to do me a favour. You know Steve Moran, the one who owes me money?'

'You speak of little else these days.'

'Well, Charlie has offered to lean on him. Frighten him, I suppose.'

'Good idea.'

'I'm beginning to regret it.'

'Perhaps I could borrow him for an afternoon or two? I have several writers I'd like "sorted out".'

'You always did like to bear a grudge.'

'Yes, although initially I like to nurture them like a prize anthurium. And even if you lose a bit of interest in the watering and feeding, they last forever. Anything else?'

'Well . . . no . . . Never mind.' Nick wasn't quite ready to share his medical situation with Sam. There would be time for all that. He hoped.

5

A few days later Nick was looking through the journals Kitty had given him, handwritten in an elegant, flowing script. Entries recording all her stage, television and film performances were recorded in great detail along with a number of waspish comments about some of her fellow actors. *RN's entrance is more Peaseblossom than Henry V* and *Our director is such a windbag he lights up a room just by leaving it.* The journals and diaries also contained some correspondence to Kitty. A brief note on Basildon Bond writing paper in green ink caught his eye.

My dearest Kitty

The play is going swimmingly. Only slightly discommoded by the stage manager's remark that that the colour of my shoes is all wrong for the character. You must come down to the Royal Court before the shade of my footwear ends our run.

Johnny

Other letters were more difficult to read. Copying the material would be a painstaking job, but invaluable. Nick had tried on more than one occasion to decipher scrawled notes from subjects whose ideas had come to them suddenly and who were too lazy to commit them to a computer. On the other hand, some elderly subjects just didn't own electronic equipment, and everything was done in dictation – sometimes at the other end of a telephone.

Of course, his subjects differed greatly. Junior Hamilton gave him a lot. He had had the idea of an autobiography while he was still playing, and during training sessions would speak into the digital recorder hidden in his track suit, much to the amusement of his teammates and consternation of the gaffer. Celebrity autobiographies usually originated from agents or publishers, but this one had come from Junior himself. Junior had wanted to tell his 'rags-to-riches' story and show kids from similarly humble backgrounds that they too could achieve something. However, most of all he'd done it for his parents, who when he was a boy had devoted much of their lives to driving him all over London to junior league matches and then watching and supporting him as he progressed into various academy teams all over the country.

There were, of course, times when the footballer had led Nick a merry dance. Pinning him down to a particular day or time was never easy. Once, Nick had invited him to stay the night at his flat so they could do some work that evening and then make an early start the following day. Junior had arrived as expected, but announced that he'd met someone on the train and now had a date that evening. 'She might have a fit mother,' Junior had replied when Nick protested. 'We could double-date.' Two days were lost at the Grenadian Embassy when he and Junior planned to meet at Heathrow before he was flying off on holiday to Dubai, only to discover that Junior had no passport. 'Oh, man – the club usually took care of that sort of thing.' Nick had developed a genuine fondness for Junior's candour and kindness, but by the end of their collaboration, and after Junior had messed him around so many times, and wasted so much of Nick's time, he had texted Nick, *You must have wanted to kill me?*

If I hadn't liked you so much, Nick texted back, *I probably would have done.*

Steve Moran had been quite forthcoming, and provided him with reams of self-recorded material, expecting an immediate response until it was time for the money; Charlie Robertson, initially pretty cagey and ensuring that Nick knew exactly what was on and off the record, surprisingly helpful, although he didn't like being recorded, and all the notes were handwritten. The interviews were always conducted at Charlie's home, and always began with a chat about Nick's personal life. Frankie had given him very little from the beginning – in fact, was still giving very little. He was probably still in the pub with his groupies.

In a deliberate act of prevarication, Nick decided to ring his GP. Advised that he was number 14 in the queue he typed Ashley Robertson's name into Google and searched under 'Images,' but found only the one photograph Charlie had given him of the two of them at Ascot. Well, at least he could tell Charlie he'd tried. He asked Alexa, who suggested an American actress, a local DIY outlet and a retired darts player. If he didn't make progress he could forget the five grand advance on Steve's money. He certainly didn't want to antagonise the man. Then Nick checked his Amazon page, which he hadn't done for at least two days, to see how sales of his various books were progressing. He usually received a percentage of the royalties, so it mattered.

Despite the poor pay – he once worked out that he had received one tenth of the minimum wage for a year's work on a project – he couldn't give it up. It was the only way he could scratch a living now, and besides, there was the lure of being flung into yet another subject's life. Whenever one of his books was published, there was a feeling of accomplishment, even if he hadn't really accomplished anything.

There were times when he even enjoyed the actual writing. Some would-be (mainly amateur) authors required a shed at the end of the garden with a view of rolling hills and seascapes before they could write. Nick followed the school of Truman Capote, Patricia Highsmith and Marcel Proust of working in bed with food, alcohol and cigarettes – well, not cigarettes, as he had given up smoking in 1973 when he realised looking cool with a Gitanes hanging from his bottom lip wasn't going to attract women after all.

Then there were the writers who followed certain rituals. John Cheever would put on a sharp suit, catch the lift to the basement to a storage room, strip down to boxer shorts and spend the morning there writing. Nick's was not so much a ritual as lying in his bed, attired in his 1920s-style velvet bed-jacket, occasionally lapsing into a Noel Coward impersonation, laptop resting gently on his loins until it became too hot. Maybe the cause of his prostate cancer? He'd have a word with the GP when he finally he got through. There might be a chance of a paid article for the *BMJ*.

Some authors liked to start early in the morning and knock off as soon as they'd completed the required amount of words for the day. Nick was more pragmatic: wrote as much as possible at any time day or night until he dropped off. Actually, he wouldn't mind a snooze now . . .

'You are number twelve in the queue.'

There was a knock at the door. It was his neighbour Grace.

'Oh, hi.' Nick indicated his mobile.

Grace raised her hands apologetically. 'I can come back later?' She seemed a little perturbed, which was unlike her.

'No, it's OK. I'm trying to contact my GP. I'm number twelve in the queue.'

'Nothing serious?'

Nick shook his head and cleared some papers off the sofa so Grace could sit down. 'It's not about the Spurs shirt for Marcel, is it? Junior will sort it out, I promise. He always comes through, after a lot of nagging.'

'No, Marcel's fine about it. I didn't like to ask you the other day at the Crematorium, but . . . I need a huge favour. It's about one of my clients. An asylum seeker from Iran. He's in trouble with the government. He'd be in danger if he ever went back, and he needs somewhere to stay.'

'Ah.'

'You see, asylum seekers are usually hosted by the Home Office, but they're often housed miles away. He's refused Home

Office accommodation up north. It will be easier to help Danesh if he's in London.'

'Where is he now?'

'In a hostel, but he has to leave. At home, in Iran, he was studying medicine.'

'Well . . .' Given his medical condition, Nick was thinking, this Danesh might come in handy . . . 'I'm not sure. The spare bedroom is tiny, and full of clutter.'

'It would only be for a short time.'

'Things are a bit hectic at the moment.'

'Oh, well. Thought I'd ask.'

'And you can't have him, Grace?'

'No, it's not a good idea, and I can't think of anyone else.' Grace was staring imploringly at Nick. Her usual authoritative manner had softened.

Nick stared back. 'I've never seen you give me that look before. I'm quite enjoying it. Sorry, was that a bit Leslie Phillips?'

'Who?'

'Never mind.' Nick was relieved he hadn't added a '*Ding-dong!*'

'Oh, I can do better than that, Nick.' Grace looked deep into Nick's eyes and smiled.

Nick thought to himself that he wouldn't mind finding out. 'And also . . . I've got lots of work on.'

'Really?'

'Don't be so surprised. Too much. But I don't have much choice, to be honest.'

'I hope you don't mind me asking this.' Grace hesitated. 'But — did you ever want to be a *proper* writer? Plays, novels?'

'You sound like my agent. Well, I do actually consider myself a proper writer, Grace.'

'I didn't mean to . . .'

'It's a question I've been asked lots of times. Anyway, these autobiographies are mostly my own work. And there's quite a lot of embellishment. Some of them are works of pure fiction. And I have done other things. Writing for radio used to be my forte, but the commissions dried up.'

His mobile interrupted with, 'You are number twelve in the queue.'

'Oh, for goodness' sake. Still number twelve!' He turned to Grace. 'What's taking number eleven so long?'

Grace smiled. 'I think you'll find it's the person at number one that's holding you up.'

'Oh. Mathematics was never my strong point.' Nick had had enough and rang off. He decided it was time to change the subject, but didn't want Grace to go. 'So . . . how did you get into your work? *Windrush?*'

Grace looked at him with a little frustration. 'That's the question *I've* been asked lots of times. Not every person of colour has *Windrush* connections. But I do have family connections with another boat. The SS *Rowan*. My great grandfather was a saxophonist in the Southern Syncopated Orchestra. He was born in Barbados, and joined the band in New York 1919.'

Nick looked blank. 'I'm afraid I've never heard of them.'

'They were well regarded. And most well-known for bringing black musicians to the UK. Most of them from the Caribbean or America. Sidney Bechet was a member.'

'And the boat connection?'

'That's the tragic part. The orchestra played in Glasgow, but on their way to Dublin in 1921 for their next engagement, their passenger ship – that's the *Rowan* – sank. Thirty-six people drowned, including nine of the orchestra. My great-grandfather survived and settled in Kennington. And the rest is family history.'

'And that was the end of the orchestra?'

'Pretty much. The survivors came back to Glasgow and charities helped replace their instruments. I think they played a couple more times, but they disbanded about a year later. Really sad. They were ahead of their time – there were even three women in the orchestra.' Grace hesitated for a moment. 'Hey, maybe there's a book in this for you?'

People were always suggesting ideas to Nick for books, and this did sound fascinating. He certainly wouldn't mind working with Grace. But the thought of all that research...

'Don't worry, I wasn't really serious. Listen, I'd better let you get on.'

'Let me think about your refugee. I know what Ben's answer will be.'

'Thank you, Nick. I really appreciate that.' Grace held Nick's hands in hers for a little longer than necessary.

When Grace had left, Nick felt a little unsettled. Not so much about helping her out, but that she had never shown so much interest in his life. He didn't think it was just because she needed a favour. Perhaps... perhaps... no, she couldn't possibly be interested in him. But she definitely seemed to be flirting with him. Possibly. He wondered why he had never noticed what a seductive, mellifluous voice she possessed. And some of those looks she had been giving him . . .

Or was it all in his imagination? It was all a bit confusing, and he had enough confusion in his life at the moment.

On the way to Deirdre's Nick rang his agent.

'Oh, hello, Nick, it's Clarissa here.'

'I did ask to speak to Graham.'

'Graham's still in Mauritius. How are you?'

'Pissed off.'

'Oh. Not like you,' she added somewhat unnecessarily.

'Steve Moran. I still haven't had the first payment and the book is out.'

'Have you tried ringing him?'

Nick's exasperation had been exacerbated by his quickened step, and he had become increasingly breathless. 'Of course I've tried ringing him. But isn't that your job?'

'Yes, OK, OK.'

'Otherwise, I might have to take matters into my own hands.'

'I can barely hear you, Nick. You're very out of breath. Are you having sex, Nick? Are you . . . calling me while you're at it?'

Nick thought he could hear a guffaw in the background. 'Clarissa, I'm not having sex. I have a Freedom Pass and a Senior Railcard instead. What I don't have is any money.'

'All right, Nick, all right. I'm afraid the line is breaking up. If you're not having sex, you need to see a doctor about that wheezing. Bye.'

Clarissa flung her mobile to the bottom of the bed and threw off the sheet. 'Where were we?'

Junior Hamilton clasped his hands behind his head and lay back. 'I think you were about to check my proofs, babe.'

'Oh, I think we're past that stage,' Clarissa murmured as she drew herself closer. 'It's time to work on that sequel.'

It was the occasional silences that Nick sometimes found hard to tolerate. A sort of aggressive/passive state he and the normally genial Deirdre often found themselves in while wanting to outdo the other in some kind of competitive avoidance. He looked around yet again. Exactly the sparsely furnished, impersonalised room he had expected before his first visit several months ago, from which nothing could gleaned of the therapist's private life. Walls magnolia, no family photographs, a select library of psychoanalysis tomes filling a pine Ikea bookcase, an unhealthy cheese plant in the corner beneath a nondescript, bucolic watercolour. A box of tissues on the coffee table that separated the two armchairs. He had presumed there would be a photograph of Freud, a watercolour of Jung or a framed letter from Melanie Klein, but of these there were none. Instead, to his continuing surprise, a print of Edvard Munch's *The Scream* next to the window. When he had asked Deirdre why such an inappropriate image adorned the wall, she had only smiled enigmatically. He was determined to find out – there must be some deep psychological explanation. Perhaps it was there precisely to provoke a response.

Meanwhile this particular silence had run its course. 'We

talked briefly about Amy last time,' said Deirdre. 'I really don't think you've come to terms with her death. You said you were going to bring in a letter from her?'

'Oh, yes.' Nick retrieved the letter from his jacket pocket wishing he'd never mentioned it.

Deirdre unfolded the letter, but after reading a few lines shook her head. 'What's this?' She handed it back to Nick. 'A letter from the hospital? Nick, this is serious. Are you sure you don't want to talk about *this*?'

'Ah. No. Wrong letter. It was a mistake.'

'Mmm. Maybe an unconscious mistake?' Deirdre raised an eyebrow.

'No, no, no. I'm not ready yet.'

Deirdre looked at Nick curiously. 'Were you going to tell me about this?'

Nick was becoming flustered. 'At some stage. Later on. But not now.' He handed over the letter he had intended to give to Deirdre, who reached for her glasses and began to scan the pages. 'Would you mind reading it aloud?'

'Mmm ... This is an unusual request, Nick. And it's quite long.'

'Please. Please. It would help me re-process the feelings. As you might say.'

Deirdre appeared doubtful. 'Oh. OK.' She put on her glasses. "Dear Nick, I miss you—"'

'Hah!' This was Nick's usual response to the first line of the missive.

'"—I realise I hurt you so much. I didn't really know what I was doing. My head was all over the place. I never really loved Mike – not like I loved you. It's something I regret doing every day. If only..."'

Yeah, yeah, yeah, Nick thought. Of course, he had read the letter a hundred times, and it was only when it came to the part when Amy begged to come back that he felt anything. Perhaps he should have agreed for Ben's sake – if only for the limited time she had left.

'"I guess those days in Los Angeles were something else. Hard to recapture..."'

Nick's thoughts wandered.

It was true, of course. Nick had been selling sandwiches along Main Street in Santa Monica when he met Amy, who worked in a bookstore. She ordered an avocado, tomato and bean sprout on sourdough. She loved his Englishness, his shyness, his politeness. He loved her looks. After a few more encounters he gave her a discount and moved into her studio apartment on the Venice Beach boardwalk. Pre-gentrified Venice was a dangerous place to live: regular shootings, robberies, random gang violence. Not to mention wayward and stoned skateboarders.

He fell in love with her spontaneity, her free-spirited lifestyle. Rules were there to be broken. She had been fined several times for smoking joints or drinking wine at the beach ... and indulging in both while topless. The bliss was sometimes temporarily soured by her regular pronouncements that their relationship was 'bourgeois' and that they should conduct an open relationship.

Nick had had an obsession with America as long as he could

remember, snuggling down under the sheets with his radio tuned to American Forces Network, listening to baseball or American football. It didn't matter which sport and whether he knew what the fuck was going on: he loved the energy, the tone and most of all the accents, which he emulated. The atmosphere — even over the radio — was intoxicating. It was as if he was eating chilli dogs and drinking grape soda while the cheers and boos reverberated from his headphones.

His love affair with the US had continued through the Seventies. While at university he had travelled across the States in an agency car — five of them in a Ford Mustang that was only meant for a driver and two passengers. The car, belonging to a Mrs Shimmel from Scarsdale, was to be delivered to her son, a record producer in Laurel Canyon. She had loaded it with toilet rolls and household goods, and so embarrassed was the younger Shimmel by his mother's antics that he had presented Nick, whose birthday it was, with a number of joints. 'Welcome to California.' Nick knew he was going to enjoy life in the Golden State.

He had returned to the City of Angels in 1980, determined to experience LA lifestyle to 'the max'. He had no far-fetched dreams of selling scripts to Hollywood moguls — the nearest he came was selling a turkey with Swiss cheese and coleslaw on wholewheat to Arnold Schwarzenegger and chatting regularly to Bob Dylan, who was rehearsing his band in a building along Nick's route. He was working illegally selling lunches to shops and businesses in Santa Monica — illegal because he shouldn't have been working, but also because the sandwiches were being made in the kitchen on his ironing board. The Santa Monica Health Department would have had more than a passing interest in the fact that he was slicing bread on the board recently vacated by his boxer shorts.

His route along Main Street was varied. Dorothy Winkler ran a gift shop and never bought anything, but her cutting, whiplash humour was a bright spot. Any gossip was greeted by her with, 'Well, I'll be dipped in shit.' On occasion she would shorten it to 'Well, I'll be dipped,' a phrase Nick had adopted for general use. Dorothy introduced him to a friend visiting from New York, 'Mario', only for Nick to discover the following day that this was Mario Puzo of *Godfather* fame. 'Well, I'll be dipped,' was all he was able to say.

Cheyenne, the receptionist and masseuse at the Acupressure Workshop, came so close to buying a sandwich, but there would always be a hitch — either too many positive ions in the air, or too few, or her chakras were so far up the spout that 'If I ate anything in the next twenny-four hours, I could honestly *die*?' But Nick never gave up on her, just in case her ying and yang were ever perfectly in tune for an egg salad on rye.

Fortunately there were regular customers too. The guys who represented the Sparkletts singing group who reminisced about Sixties LA when, if it was a particularly 'pretty day', meetings would be cancelled at short notice so the sunshine and blue skies at the beach could be properly appreciated; the pushy realtor (chicken salad on raisin bread) who every time he called on her asked Nick if he was interested in buying a 'a piece of property'. He had given up the pleading of poverty to which she was clearly immune and finally promised he would talk to his parents about this unique investment possibility.

'Nick, are you listening?' Deirdre had removed her glasses.

'Yes. Of course.'

'Well, it didn't look like it. What were you thinking about?'

'Um . . . Sandwiches, actually.' Nick shifted uncomfortably.

'Sandwiches.'

'Yes.'

'It's interesting to me that you were thinking about something like sandwiches and not your late wife.'

'Well, I . . .'

'Sometimes I think you're a bit of a fraud.'

'That's a bit harsh!'

'Here's a little trade secret. Have you heard of Fritz Perls?'

Nick considered for a moment. Was he the frontman for the Dead Kennedys?

'He was a renowned psychoanalyst,' Deirdre was continuing, 'who would confront his more resistant patients in an attempt to obtain a reaction. He could be rude, and even insult them, to elicit some kind of emotional response.'

'Is that what you're doing now?'

'I repeat, I think you are a bit of a fraud.'

'Well . . .' Nick hesitated. 'Maybe I am.'

6

Richard Greenwood had spoken to Nick about ghosting Cecil Kett's book, but been told his son was inundated with work and had to say no. Nick had suggested that his father take the project on. 'I'm sure you could make a go of it, Dad. You've already established a relationship with Cecil. It's all about trust.'

Richard was intrigued by the idea. Cecil hadn't seemed disappointed when Richard told him Nick was too busy, and had reluctantly agreed to Richard helping him out. 'I s'pose I might need help with the odd word.'

'It's all about trust, Cecil,' Richard replied.

So, soon after their meeting in the supermarket, Richard found himself at Cecil Kett's home. The name carved in driftwood on the outside of the cottage, 'Fort Apache', should have given him a heads-up on the interior décor. He looked around the room, which was a mass of Native American memorabilia and iconography. Framed posters depicted braves in canoes, and a spectacularly large photograph in a gilt frame of Chief Red Cloud in war paint and extravagant feather headdress hung over the fireplace. In the corner, dominating the room and reaching the ceiling, was a cigar-store Indian.

'My goodness, Cecil. That's quite a statement. All that's missing is a totem pole.'

'Funny you should say that. I ordered one from the same website for the front garden. Don't mention it if the missus comes back. Not keen.'

'No, no, of course not.' Richard could see her point of view. He opened his notebook, took out his favourite Parker pen and decided to go straight in. 'So. How long ago did you discover you were of Red Indian stock?'

'We are Native Americans. We'd better get that straight from the start.'

'Yes, of course.' Richard was already irritated.

'Words are powerful. We cannot be judged by the colour of our skin.'

Richard stared at Cecil's wan complexion. He refrained from telling him he looked more like a paleface.

'I'm a proud member of Red Power. We want self-determination to control our lands and resources. We embarked upon a of a campaign of civil disobedience.'

'Such as?'

'The protest in 2016 about the Dakota Access pipeline. It was going to run through Standing Rock reservation. Land belonging to the Lakota Sioux.' Cecil's eyes blazed with emotion. 'We created a blockade against an onslaught of batons, tear gas and rubber bullets. A lot of protesters went to prison. And before that was the occupation of Wounded Knee to commemorate the massacre of 1890. Hundreds of the Lakota tribe were killed by the Seventh Cavalry.'

Richard feigned interest. 'Fascinating.'

'I can't bear that man.'

'Who?'

'George Custer. They made him out to be a hero in the films. Especially that one with Errol Flynn. Well, he got his comeuppance.'

'Errol Flynn?'

'No, George Custer. Richard, if we're going to write my story, it's got to be truthful, honest and historically correct.'

'Of course. No forked tongues.' Richard was rather pleased with that.

'Are you trying to be funny, Richard?'

'No!' Richard looked appropriately guilty. 'Just trying to capture your voice, as we say in the trade.'

'Well, not a very good start. I'll forgive you this once. But before we begin, can I ask you one thing?'

'Of course.'

'Why are you wearing tissue boxes on your feet?'

'Dad, I don't see how you can even think twice about it. Danesh — that's his name, isn't it, Grace?'

Grace nodded.

'He's desperate! He's in danger for speaking up against the regime!'

'I know, Ben,' said Nick. 'I'd like to help this man, but we barely have any space for ourselves.'

'We can make the lounge into a spare bedroom. We can manage.'

Nick, Grace and Ben were sitting around the Greenwoods' kitchen table. Nick had told Ben briefly about Grace's request the previous evening, but it was agreed that Grace would come around this evening to fill in the details.

'Oh, Ben, it's going to be very disruptive.'

'Disruptive!' Ben was becoming flustered. 'Yeah, right. Not as disruptive as leaving his home in Iran and family having to cross continents, braving the English Channel in a rowing boat, and then sleeping rough.'

Grace was looking more and more ill at ease. 'Look, perhaps I should leave you two to talk about Danesh.' Maybe she had made a mistake about approaching Nick. She liked him and he seemed an empathetic guy, but perhaps she had misread the situation. Not often she did that. It obviously wasn't a good idea. She would have to think of something else. 'And Marcel is getting fed up.'

'Grace, Marcel is quite happy on his iPad. Aren't you, Marcel?'

'Yes.' Marcel didn't look up.

'Come on, Marcel, let's go.'

'No, I . . . I . . . like it here. Anyway.' Marcel was still engrossed.

'Grace, please stay. It's helpful having you here.' Nick knew she would be more reasonable than his son. 'How long might it be for?'

'Difficult to tell. But you could ask Danesh to leave whenever you want.'

'Yes, but once he's here, it will be difficult to . . . Look, has he had a security check?'

'Dad! So that's it: you think he's a terrorist or a spy.'

'It's OK, Ben. It's a fair question for your dad to ask. And the answer is yes. He has security clearance. I wouldn't ask you otherwise.'

'We only have one bathroom.'

'So, a man might be sent back to be tortured because you need to take a dump in private?'

'I'm just being practical. It will affect you too. You won't be able to play your music at such a volume. Could bring on his PTSD.'

'He doesn't have PTSD,' said Grace. 'I think you're both getting a little over-dramatic.'

Nick turned to Grace. 'Can he contribute anything?'

'He receives forty pounds a week in subsistence.'

'That's not going to go far.'

'It doesn't,' Grace said. 'And he isn't allowed to work.'

Ben was horrified. 'That's ridiculous!'

They both looked at Nick, who threw his hands up in defeat. 'All right. For a week's trial period and see how it goes.'

'Thanks, Nick. I'm very grateful. Let me ring Danesh.' Grace got up. 'Come on, Marcel.' When his mum gave him the look Marcel knew he was on his way home.

Ben was delighted not only at the thought of coming to Danesh's aid, but also at getting one over on his dad. 'What does he eat, Grace? I'll do the cooking.'

Nick gazed at his son. 'You don't think he's suffered enough?'

Later that evening, Nick sat down with Ben to watch a recording of Steve Moran's final appearance in *The Southerners*.

'I hate soaps,' said Ben.

'It's only one scene I want to watch. He's been sacked. No one could bear working with him any longer.'

'Oh, the guy who owes you money?'

Nick fast-forwarded to the end of the episode. Steve Moran aka Eddie Dunn was facing down a couple of villains who were out to get him.

> THUG 1: Hello, Eddie, seems you've served yourself up on a plate. You can't come back to the street and play happy families.
>
> EDDIE: If I could turn back the clock, I would.
>
> THUG 1: Not this time, Eddie. This really is the end.

The second thug took out a gun and pointed it at Eddie. 'Go on!' Nick was on the edge of his seat. 'Let him have it!' Ben stared at his father. 'For fuck's sake, Dad.'

> EDDIE: You think I care? What am I losing, eh? I tried my whole life to make something of myself, and when I couldn't do it the right way, I chose the wrong way. So what? You tell Charlene I looked you in the face when you pulled the trigger. Go on. End it.

Nick buried his head in his hands. 'Yes, please. His acting is giving me a headache. Here we go . . .!'

> THUG 2: Go on, pull the trigger . . .

'Yes!' Nick was making a gun with his fingers. 'Blow him away!'

Even Ben was involved now. 'Oh, no – the gun's jammed! He's getting away!'

Nick was on his feet. 'Kill him!'

Ben gave his dad a puzzled look. 'I'm beginning to think you want him dead in real life.'

Moran jumped a wall to make his escape, but ran slap-bang into the middle of a busy road. A screech of brakes, a sickening thud, and Eddie had run under an approaching car.

'Oh, dear, he forgot his Green Cross Code.' Nick punched the air with excitement. '*Yesss!*'

'I wouldn't celebrate too much, Dad. Now he's out of the soap, you're never going to get your money.'

'Will you want sedation, Mr Greenwood?'

Nick was stretched out on a surprisingly comfortable bed, curtained off from other patients in the day hospital. 'As much as legally possible, please.'

'I've seen some men opt for no medication for this procedure.' Elsie the African nurse smiled ominously. 'Not a very good idea. I'll put in a cannula and tell the doctors.'

Nick was in for a biopsy. Funnily enough, he wasn't nervous. He was pleased to get it over with. It was on a previous appointment when the nerves had really kicked in: his hands had shaken so much he had spilt the urine sample, which had gone all over the floor, and by the time he'd finished cleaning the bathroom floor he returned to the nurse with just a few drops.

'I was going to send out a search party.' She inspected the near-empty tube. 'Is that all you could manage?'

'Stage fright, I guess.'

'You must have forgotten your lines.'

By the time he was transferred to surgery Nick was well away. Back in the recovery ward he asked Elsie when he could go home.

'When you are able to pass water. There'll be blood when you pee, but don't worry. It's normal.'

Nick was glad she'd informed him about this. He settled back and hoped he'd be able to pee soon – even if it turned into a bit of a Tarantino scene. He picked up the pad and pen he'd brought with him and attempted to work while he was waiting, but his scribbling was interrupted by a ruddy, tousle-headed man with a touch of the Jeremy Clarkson about him in the next bed, his hospital gown swinging open alarmingly as he reached over a hand. 'Biopsy?'

Before Nick could reply, the man said, 'Me too. I'm Barry. How do you do? This is my third. I'm keeping count. Like Glenn Ford in *The Fastest Gun Alive*. You see, when it comes down to medical procedures, I see each one as a bit of a gunfight.'

'Really.' Nick hoped Barry didn't have notches on his penis to prove it. And actually, Glenn Ford was a reluctant gunslinger – it was his father's character who was the gunfighter, but this didn't seem the time to correct his brother in biopsy.

'And I never have any medication.'

'Good for you.' That explained the screams Nick thought he had heard earlier.

'I don't suppose they'll find anything. They never do. I'm

actually fit as a fiddle.' Barry leaned towards Nick conspiratorially. 'I quite like hospitals. I can tell you about all the procedures.'

'I'm fine, thanks.'

'I've had them all. Endoscopy. Gastroscopy. Colonoscopy. There's not a scope I haven't had. The first endoscopy was when—'

'I'm actually trying to work.' Nick waved the pad at the man.

'What is it you do exactly?'

'I'm an author. Mainly ghostwriting.'

'Well, that is a coincidence. People have often told me I should write an autobiography. I've certainly got a story to tell. Perhaps you could help me?'

'I'm not sure, I've—'

'I'm a postman. I've seen some things on my rounds. You wouldn't believe it.'

Nick smiled. 'That's good. At least the job keeps you off the streets.'

'Oh, I haven't heard that before,' said Barry. 'Someone has already suggested a title. *Man of Letters*.'

'That's a good start. Sorry – got to go. Call of nature.' Nick stood up and hurried away.

The only call of nature Nick truly felt was to get away from Barry, but he hurried to the toilet hoping to gain some relief. It came after five minutes of patiently waiting, and it was a good job the nurse had warned him, because it was a bit of a bloodbath. But pee he did. On his return he gave Barry the thumbs-up and closed the curtains, got dressed and fled.

Ben was out, much to Nick's relief, as he didn't want to share the gory details, although he would have liked to brag to his son about how brave he had been. After a snack he poured himself a recuperative Laphroaig and worked for a couple of hours on Kitty's book, transcribing some of her letters and diary entries. He also perused the photo album Kitty had given him, which contained some images of a masked ball, Edwardian family gatherings, children on donkeys, mostly in Margate – but also photographs of soldiers. A postcard dated August 1914 was of a group of twelve men, in various relaxed poses and smiling for the camera. There was a circle in green ink around one of the men: tall, strikingly handsome with deep-set eyes and trimmed moustache, a cigarette dangling from his mouth. The postcard read,

Dearest Lily,

Splendid weather here. Still jogging along. Here I am with some of the chaps outside the cookhouse in Colchester. Off to the front tomorrow. Merry and bright as ever when I think of you.

All Love,
Hubby xxx

Nick realised he needed a pee.
The trouble was, he couldn't go.
He just couldn't go.
An hour later he still couldn't, and the pain was getting

unbearable. He tried all manner of positions and angles. He sat down on the toilet and tried to think of all the euphemisms he could for passing water.

Pointing Percy at the Porcelain.

Going to See a Man About a Dog.

Syphon the Python.

Jimmy Riddle.

Airing the Blue Vein. (Or did that mean having sex?)

None of them worked.

He just couldn't Strain the Noodle.

Nick looked at the leaflet he'd been given when he had left the hospital. *'There may be swelling after the procedure that may cause some difficulty in passing water. If you are unable to urinate eight hours after the procedure, please attend the nearest A&E department.'*

Eight hours! There were another three to go. It was the most discomfort he had ever been in. He laid down on his front. He laid on his back. He paced the flat, trying to get comfortable, for another hour. He ran the bathroom tap, hoping that *something* would bring the necessary result, when Ben came home.

'How did the biopsy go, dad?'

'Fine, thanks.'

'Why are you walking around the flat like this?'

'Just trying to get comfortable. It was a bit painful.'

'Wouldn't it be better to lie down?' Ben gave him an affectionate tap on the shoulder.

'No, it wouldn't. Please just leave me alone.'

'Only trying to help.' Ben disappeared into his room.

Nick had a hot bath, tried to immerse himself in one of

Frankie's albums, watched television, but the pain was unbearable. Finally he knocked on Ben's door. 'Ben, I'm going to have to go to hospital.'

'Again?' Ben looked concerned. 'Do you want me to come with you, Dad?'

'No, I'll get an Uber.'

By the time Nick reached A&E he was in agony and, having explained the situation and walked around the waiting room for a further hour, attracting suspicious looks from other patients, he was taken into the 'walking emergency room' and allocated a bed. After a scan of his bladder, a doctor explained that he would need a catheter to drain the urine. Nick's fears were not allayed by the raised voice followed by torturous screams of agony from the next bed, which was curtained off. Nick was able to recognise Barry's voice. Still, no time for even a little *Schadenfreude*.

A nurse who seemed young enough to be his granddaughter approached, looking more nervous than Nick. 'Don't worry about him.' She indicated the next bed. 'He's a nervous patient.'

'It's not how Glenn Ford would have reacted,' said Nick. 'Not exactly the gunslinger he said he was.'

The nurse smiled, clearly not understanding a word he'd said. 'I'm going to numb the area first with some anaesthetic gel.' She opened the packaging, her gloved hands shaking.

'Have you done this before?' Nick asked tentatively.

'Actually – no. You're my first ever catheter.' She attempted a smile.

'Me too. Good luck.'

The nurse applied the gel and prepared the catheter tube.

'Best if you look away. And take a deep breath. I know I'm going to. Well, here goes.'

Nick closed his eyes. Just my luck, he thought. Nice girl, but surely they might have found him— 'Ow, ow, *ow*!'

The nurse's hands were trembling so much that the catheter still wouldn't go in. 'Sorry. Trial and error.'

For fuck's sake, Nick thought. That's all I need. A catheter virgin.

Two more attempts followed, leaving Nick with tears of pain running down his cheeks. The nurse was equally despondent. 'I'm so sorry. I'll get my colleague. Wayne is much more experienced at this.'

'It wouldn't be hard,' Nick muttered.

She returned a few minutes later with a muscular masked nurse, pectorals bursting out of his uniform, the forearms of Crocodile Dundee and a neck the size of New South Wales. Nick took one look at him and called after the young nurse, 'Perhaps you should have another go?'

'No worries,' declared Wayne. 'I'm good at this' — and swiftly and firmly inserted the tube into Nick's shrinking penis.

Nick gasped. 'Yes, you are, aren't you?' He felt instant relief as the urine passed into the catheter bag. 'Thank you.'

And Wayne was gone like an Aussie Zorro.

The young nurse returned with a perfunctory explanation of how often the bag should be changed, and said Nick would be sent an appointment for the catheter removal in a few days when the bruising from the biopsy should have subsided. She strapped the bag to his leg. 'You can go now.'

Outside the hospital Nick was surprised to find Grace waiting for him. 'What are you doing here?'

'Ben asked me to come and collect you. He's looking after Marcel. More to the point, what are you doing here?'

'It's nothing, I'm fine.' He was the fastest gun in the West. 'I'll tell you later if you're not nice to me.'

Nick climbed into the passenger seat convinced his catheter bag would somehow come loose and flood Grace's car with urine. He clutched his leg to ensure it was stable.

'Is there something wrong with your leg?'

'No, no! Leg's fine!'

'Come on, Nick – talking can help.'

'That's why I go to my therapist.'

'You have a therapist?' Grace feigned surprise.

'Yes, I do, as a matter of fact.'

'I wouldn't have thought you were the type.'

'I didn't know you had to be a type to have a therapist.'

Grace's hand was on Nick's knee. He was a little taken aback, but mainly hoping she couldn't feel the straps to the catheter bag. 'Both hands on the wheel, please, Grace.'

She quickly removed her hand and laughed. 'What is this? My driving test?'

'The thing is,' said Nick. 'If you must know – I didn't want to blurt it out just yet – but I may have prostate cancer.'

'Oh, Nick!' Grace frowned and bit her bottom lip. 'I wasn't expecting that. I'm so sorry.' Her hand was back on his knee and this time, he realised, he wanted it to stay there. Grace stole a quick glance at him. 'You should have told me before.'

'It's a bit embarrassing. First the therapist and now this.'

'Don't be silly. And you know if there is anything I can do.'

'It's very sweet of you to give me a lift home.'

'Of course. And you really should try not to worry. It may not be cancer.'

'True,' said Nick doubtfully.

'And if you're going to get cancer, this is the one to have.'

'So they tell me.'

'You can live for years with it. If you catch it early. My brother had the same thing.'

'And what happened to him?'

'He died.'

7

'Where were we?'

'What, before you asked me to write to John Lewis, Kitty?'

Kitty nodded.

'You know it's not strictly my job.'

'I don't like emails. And while you are here I might as well make use of you. We could call it a writing exercise, to see how literary you are.' Kitty gave him an enquiring glance.

'I'm not your personal secretary.'

'Of course not. I would never have employed you.'

Although she was a tricky old bird, Nick did admire Kitty's bloody-mindedness. Of course, he had experienced difficulties with his subjects during his work as a ghostwriter, some of which had led to slanging matches and insoluble disputes. He had completed a book with a retired gay cricket umpire, who had insisted that the book be published with the title Nick had suggested, *You're Out and So Am I*. Nick had felt very pleased with himself, but the publishers had refused to bring the book out and the advance had had to be returned. A couple of subjects refused to have his name in their books at all — not even in the acknowledgements. He once had to argue the toss with a publisher who said he would only pay the advance when the book had been written and ready for publication. 'In any case,' the publisher went on in the face of Nick's protestations that 'advance' meant exactly that, 'you're not exactly going to be able to pay off your mortgage with it.' As if this was a good thing. The jacket blurb was always problematic, in that what Nick considered the essence of the book was reduced to headline-grabbing clichés, and the more important elements were sometimes edited out by over-enthusiastic editors.

So, although challenging, Kitty wasn't the most difficult subject he had ever worked with. He enjoyed being in her elegant surroundings, a change from his cramped flat. And she did have a wealth of anecdotes. 'There is a delightful story about Edith Evans. Many, in fact, but my favourite is the visit to Fortnum and Mason during the war when she was charged the exorbitant sum of nineteen shillings and sixpence for a pineapple. She handed a pound note to the assistant and declared, "Keep the change. I trod on a grape on the way in."

'Wilfred Hyde-White' – Nick was still trying to work out where to fit Dame Edith in, but Kitty was now in full flight. 'I knew him very well. Lovely man.

'Well, he was doing a tour of some dreadful farce and was in a matinée in Eastbourne. I can't remember what the play was – you'll have to look it up. Anyway, the audience mainly consisted of old ladies, who hadn't reacted to any of the jokes or set pieces. Nothing. Absolutely soul-destroying for an actor or actress doing comedy. Finally, in the second act, a snigger from the back of the stalls cut the silence like a knife. Well, dear old Wilfred, who had had quite enough of this particular audience, strode to the front of the stage and called out, "*Now* what's the matter?" Something of a bon viveur. You know he went bankrupt? At least once, I believe. He was married to—'

'This is all lovely stuff, Kitty, but perhaps we should get back to you.'

'We were in *Separate Tables* together. In fact, I have a photograph of the two of us in one of my albums. Let me fetch it while I remember.' She rose shakily out of her chair and made to cross the room.

The next thing Nick saw was Kitty flying through the air in what seemed slow motion. She landed with a sickening thud at an improbable angle on the highly polished parquet floor. There followed a tremulous groan. Nick jumped out of his seat and knelt down beside her. 'Oh, Kitty, are you all right?'

'No, of course I'm not. Does it look like it?' Kitty started wailing.

'Please, Kitty, please. I'm sure you'll be OK.'

Kitty's screams had alerted Edie, who hurried into the drawing room. 'Oh, my good gawd, what's happened to Miss Lawrence?'

'I'm afraid she's had a fall.' Nick had recovered himself a little. 'Don't move her. I'll ring for an ambulance.'

Edie fetched a cover for Kitty, whose screams had subsided into sonorous groans. It was then he noticed that wrapped around Kitty's leg was the strap of his laptop bag. Nick hurriedly sent Edie off to make Kitty a cup of tea – 'with plenty of sugar. Good for shock.'

He grasped Kitty's hand while with the other one disentangling her leg from the strap. He felt terrible, but with a bit of luck Kitty wouldn't realise it was his fault . . .

'I can see what you're doing,' the prone actress muttered. 'Why on earth did you leave the bag there?'

'I'm so sorry, Kitty. I didn't mean to be so careless.'

'You're a *bloody* fool! I knew from the start you were a useless specimen!' Her voice was raised.

The sudden outburst seemed to exhaust Kitty, who went very pale and silent. It suddenly came to Nick that he might have killed his subject. She might have struck her head. What a nightmare! He'd find it hard to forgive himself for this. He'd have to live with it *for the rest of his life. And* he'd never get her fee.

Nick thought he'd better keep Kitty talking, so the best thing was to continue asking her questions about her career. 'Tell me about Gielgud. What was he really like?' When there was no response he became very worried.

Edie had returned with the tea, and together they propped Kitty up with a pillow so she could give her small sips. Fortunately, Kitty rallied and started talking about how she had had a romance with John Gielgud, which he knew was definitely gibberish. But also a relief. Concussion was certainly better than death.

'How did it happen?' Thank goodness Edie hadn't seen the incident.

'No idea. She is very frail.'

'But she's also very careful.'

'Must have been the rug,' Nick added helpfully. He wished

he had turned the corner of the mat over as evidence. 'Yes, that must have been it. Dangerous things, rugs.'

Kitty raised her head. 'I haven't flown like that since I was in *Peter Pan* at the Old Vic.' Then she passed out.

Nick stayed until the ambulance arrived and offered to accompany Kitty to A&E. Kitty said she didn't want him anywhere near her, and to his relief asked Edie to go with her. Was their writing relationship already at an end?

The following day Nick was emptying the contents of his catheter bag when his mobile rang. He'd become quite used to the catheter – even to the extent of remarking to Ben how he'd become quite attached to it.

'Hello, Nick, it's your father.'

'Yes, Dad, your name comes up on my mobile.'

There followed a quick burst of Richard singing, 'Nobody knows the trouble I've seen.'

'This isn't the best time. In fact, I can't think of a worse time.'

'Never mind. Look, Nick, I'm having a spot of trouble with Cecil.'

'Already?'

'He doesn't seem to see my way of thinking.'

'Dad, it's his book. You have to go along with his wishes.'

'Well, I like to think of it as our book.'

'It isn't,' said Nick flatly. 'It's his book.'

'But I've come up with some marvellous ideas. I thought we could start with a prologue where Cecil is at the scene of the Wounded Knee battleground. He's just applied his warpaint, thrusts his lance into the ground and swears vengeance on the white man. In the Lakotan language, of course. Then he mounts an Appaloosa horse and rides off into the sunset.'

'Did this actually happen?'

'Of course not. He can't speak Lakotan.'

'But did he go to Wounded Knee?'

'I thought it set the scene.'

'And I'm right in thinking Cecil didn't like the idea?'

'Yes. I mean, no, he didn't. Said it was a load of poppycock. But I've told him it's got to stay in.'

'Dad, you can't do that. Look, let's talk about it another time.'

'How about this for a title? *Reservation for One*.'

'Dad, do you need some help with this?'

'I wouldn't mind, Nick, but I know how busy you are.'

'It's OK. I don't want to see you get yourself in a pickle. Tell Cecil Kett that I'll talk to him and maybe between the three of us we can work something out. Now, I've got to go, there's something I need to watch on television. Call you later.' Nick hung up abruptly and swapped his mobile for the remote.

He was just in time for the live edition of *Midday Chat*. Not a show he would normally watch, but today Penny Bliss, the once glamorous, now slightly chubby presenter, was glowing with excitement as she addressed the studio audience, 'You know him as Eddie Dunn, the bad boy, who last night came to a bad end in our favourite TV soap.' She conducted the adoring audience in the obligatory '*Ahhh*.'

'Shame it was only on TV,' Nick muttered.

'And he *was* a bad boy, wasn't he?' Penny continued. The

audience whooped and the other presenters, ex-*Emmerdale* actress Sally Hardie and the controversial agony aunt Bernice Joseph, nodded excitedly. 'And didn't we love him for that. Yeah? Here he is to talk about his candid new autobiography, *A Scouse La*', which is out this Friday,' and she waved a copy of the book at the audience. 'Please welcome Steve Moran!'

Steve Moran emerged from behind the stage to much applause and hollering, grinning and waving at the audience. He hugged each member of the team in turn, clinging on to Bernice Joseph a little too long, to her obvious discomfort.

'Here's my first question,' Nick shouted furiously at the screen. 'Where's Nick Greenwood's money, Steve?'

Penny seemed not to hear Nick's suggestion, and made a calming motion towards the audience. 'Whoa now – I don't think we've ever had such a reaction, have we, girls?' Finally, a frantic calm prevailed, and Penny turned to her guest. 'So, Steve. Your autobiography. We can't wait. What's in it?' She smiled teasingly at Moran.

As Moran returned her gaze his brilliant white teeth lit up the studio. 'Absolutely everything, Penny!'

'And absolutely none of it is true,' yelled Nick, 'you talentless wanker!'

'Well, I've actually read it,' gushed Sally Hardie, 'and it's *brilliant*!' Moran feigned embarrassment at the shattering applause.

'Tell me, Steve' – Bernice had her serious face on – 'did you have any help writing the book?'

Steve shook his head. 'I decided against that. Everyone has a different version of events and memories, and I wanted this to be *my* story.'

'You're going to say you wrote every word!' screamed Nick.

Steve Moran was straight-faced sincerity. 'I wrote every word. That was really important for me, you know?'

'The *bastard!*'

The living room door opened on a suspicious-looking Ben. 'Who are you talking to, Dad?'

'No-one.'

'You talking to the TV?'

Nick indicated his mobile. 'Of course not.'

'You are so weird sometimes.'

Nick's call went to Moran's answer message. 'Hi Steve. It's Nick, your non-existent ghostwriter here. How are you? Well, I know how you are because I'm watching you live on TV right now, lying through your shiny white veneers. Which I don't really care about as much as I care about you not paying me the *money* you owe me for making your *miserably* dull life *marginally* more interesting than watching you *act*. Except for watching your death on TV last night, which I must say I *really enjoyed*, and which I'm hoping was just a rehearsal for the *real thing*.'

'Come on, Marcel. Breakfast is ready,' Grace called out from the kitchen, a little impatient that at the third time of asking he had still not appeared. She walked down the hallway and entered his bedroom, where she found him curled up in bed.

'Marcel, what's going on? Why aren't you dressed? Aren't you feeling well?'

'Don't want to go school today.' Marcel turned to face the wall.

Grace sat down on the bed. 'Marcel!'

He reluctantly shifted to face his mother. 'Not going, M-mum.'

'You love school! And all your friends will be expecting you.'

'I don't care, anyway.'

'Marcel, I have to go to work. We're going to be late.'

'Not going.'

'I haven't got time for this.'

'I want to play FIFA with B-ben.'

'Ben's at college.'

'I'll play on my own.'

'Just get up, Marcel.' Marcel did not respond as Grace's tone grew sterner. Instead, he buried his head under the bedclothes.

'What's wrong?' Grace attempted to pull gently at the duvet.

'It's Eddie.'

'Who's Eddie?'

'Eddie Dunn, of course!' Marcel sat up. 'He was bad but my favourite in *Southerners*.'

'Oh, Marcel, how many times have I told you that it's not real?'

'I know that. Mum. But it's still making me sad.' Marcel took a deep breath. 'Is that what happened to m... my dad?'

'No, you know it isn't. We've talked about this so many times. You know he wanted to go away and do other things with his life.'

'Without me?'

'Yes, without both of us. Look, Marcel, I really need to—'

'My dad's not here, so he's dead, like Eddie is.'

'Oh, Marcel, this a very big thing. Can we please talk about it again tonight when we have more time?'

Marcel looked thoughtful. 'P . . . p . . . romise?'

'Of course. You know I've never broken a promise to you.'

Marcel swung his feet around the side of the bed and cuddled his mother, 'I love you, Mum. You're the best mum I ever had.'

'Well, that's a relief. And I love you too, Marcel. Now we really need to get going.'

While Grace was discussing life-and-death issues with Marcel, Nick was on a train to Kent to see Frankie. On the way there, worried about Kitty's welfare, he telephoned a very frosty Edie. Kitty, she informed him, was now on an orthopaedic ward, having fractured her hip in the fall. On no account should he try and visit her, Edie went on, and it was unlikely that her employer would want to continue with the book. Of course, Nick did try and contact the hospital ward, and requested that the nurse pass on his good wishes.

Nick had decided to visit Frankie at his house, thinking that at least his subject would be a captive audience and maybe more relaxed in his own home. Bedford Falls, a converted barn in Kent a few miles from the picturesque village of Chilham, was somewhat off the beaten track. 'Even the Old Bill don't know this place exists,' Frankie explained. 'That's come in handy a few times.' According to Frankie the local community welcomed him as 'a proper local'. He was also proud of the name he had given to his abode. 'A tribute to my favourite film. Always leaves me blubbing like a fucking baby.'

Inside the front door Nick was greeted by an impressive row of platinum discs along the opposite wall, not to mention portraits of Frankie with the various rock stars with whom he'd worked. There was Frankie and Rod Stewart playing darts at the King's Head pub in Santa Monica, Frankie and a couple of members of Deep Purple outside the Albert Hall, and a faded image of Frankie and Dolly Parton – Frankie couldn't remember the venue or whether he had actually performed with Dolly, but it was a 'fabulous night'. And then there were the guitars – wall-to-wall Gibsons, Martins and Fenders in various gleaming hues. It appeared that Frankie took care of his instruments better than he cared for himself. There were numerous pictures of his stunning ex-wives in various states of undress dotted around the open-plan living space. Nick was never sure quite how much interest to take in these portraits. To observe closely would seem prurient, but too little attention would seem somehow rude. Frankie didn't seem to mind either way. From some chat with him it seemed wife number four, 'Franny', had departed to live with a merchant banker on the Côte d'Azur – something he had omitted to tell Lucy – though Frankie seemed sure she would return to Bedford Falls once she got bored with him.

Frankie had welcomed Nick with an industrial-strength double espresso and motioned to the leopard-print sofa. The guitarist seemed in high spirits. 'Great to see you, man. I've got some news for you.'

Nick was hoping that Frankie had actually remembered something and written it down before his memory failed him. But no. 'In fact,' Frankie continued, 'there are a couple of things that I'm excited about.' He proceeded to remove his shades. 'I've been in touch with Bruce and Dec from Aslan's Roar. We're re-forming.'

'That is great news.' Nick was already weighing up the advantages and disadvantages; Frankie might be able to pick up some anecdotes from his old pals, but it would mean he would be even more distracted from the book and Nick might be chasing him all around the country.

'We've already got some dates, and we're going to start rehearsing in a couple of weeks. We're going to call the tour "Aslan's Roar Reborn".' It was a good thing C. S. Lewis was long in his grave, Nick thought.

'The guys are coming here to the studio. I've started writing some new material. I think working on the book has started a new creative urge.'

'Really?' Nick hadn't noticed.

'I want to thank you for all the work you've done. I do appreciate it, you know. You've been fucking great.' Frankie nodded theatrically as if agreeing with himself.

Nick was genuinely touched. For all the frustrations of working with Frankie, he realised he had become quite fond of the man. 'Thanks, Frankie. I hope it goes well. And what's the other news?'

'I'm going to sell the copyright of my songs.'

'Oh?'

'They'll bring in some dosh – it's expensive to run this place on my own now that Franny's gone.' He glanced wistfully at a super-sized painting of a woman in a leather bikini. Lucy, despite being a beautifully spiritual presence, didn't contribute a penny to the bills. 'And the good news is that I'm going to give you first offer. You can have the whole lot for two hundred grand.'

Nick stared back.

'Thought you'd be pleased. Believe me, that's a deal. I discussed it with Lucy. The whole back catalogue for under a quarter of a mill is not to be sniffed at.'

'I'm sorry, Frankie. I'm very flattered, but I haven't got that sort of money.'

Frankie looked crestfallen. 'I could go to a hundred and seventy-five if that would help?'

'Look, Frankie, the advance between us for your book was ten thousand, and we've only had half of that so far. And unless we finish this book, we're not going to receive the second half. In any case, I wouldn't know how to do you justice and make my money back. It would be better for you to sell your rights to an established music publishing company.'

'Tried that. No-one's interested.'

'I thought you said I was first on the list?'

'Did I?' Not for the first time in his life, Frankie looked blank.

'Whatever. Let's do some work.'

'Yeah. How does a hundred grand sound?'

A couple of hours later Nick was on the train back to London. He'd arranged a meeting with Grace and Danesh that evening, but first he had another, even more important appointment.

Steve Moran's book launch was due to take place at Scrimshaws, a large West End store. Established in 1787, its customers over the years had included King George III, Oscar Wilde and Tyson Fury. A pretty good place to shift some copies, and the chance to have a word with Moran.

Nick walked past the Ritz and Fortnum's, home of the celebrated food department and the famous clock where four-foot figures of Mr Fortnum and Mr Mason make their appearance on the hour. He loved this part of town, preferring a slow stroll rather than the jostling hordes of 'customers' at Piccadilly Circus. Every district in London had its own character and charm, and St James's was no different. He'd become intrigued by this area when a cousin doing some family research had discovered that George Greenwood, a retired butcher, had lived in Bury Street. Further investigation had unearthed a family member residing in nearby Mayfair in the eighteenth century. Nick had become excited at the thought of his great-great-great-grandfather occupying a home at the prestigious Mount Street address. It was to his considerable disappointment that 103 Mount Street turned out to be the local workhouse. Ben, however, was delighted to come from such humble beginnings, and reminded his father at every opportunity when Nick became a little too smug about his ancestral background.

Charles Farlow had opened his first shop on the Strand in 1840, and those seeking finest country wear and shooting accessories had been visiting since. Of course, Nick wasn't exactly the hunting-shooting-fishing type, but he loved the history of the shop. London watchmakers Backes and Strauss had been trading since 1789, and Royal hatters James Lock and Co. had been placing hats on Royal bonces a century earlier. In a nearby shop too posh to have a name a suit of armour was stretched out on the floor, and a sales assistant was putting the pieces together like a medieval jigsaw. Nick liked to pop into the James J. Fox cigar shop and imbibe the aroma of their wares, although he had never smoked a cigar in his life. He strolled up Jermyn Street, where Beau Brummell's bronze statue was located. 'To be truly elegant', the plinth read, 'one should not be noticed.' Nick was going to make sure he was noticed tonight. To give him a little Dutch courage, he decided to have a couple of drinks at the historic Chequers tavern in Duke Street, a haunt of coachmen in the eighteenth century. After a pint and a large Glenlivet he wandered down the alleyway of Crown Passage. Not that he needed it, but he thought he might have another whisky or two at the Red Lion, 'London's oldest village inn'.

Nick arrived at Scrimshaws in good time, though somewhat the worse for wear, for the 7 o'clock start. At the back of the shop a crowd was gathering, and the staff were trying to organise two queues: one where the copies of *A Scouse La'* could be bought, and another in front of a desk where the books would be signed. Nick looked all around, but there was no sign of Steve Moran, or anyone he knew from the publishers. He accosted a harassed-looking middle-aged male sales assistant whose name tag read 'Norman', and who seemed to be in charge. 'What time is Steve Moran arriving, Norman?'

'He should have been here half an hour ago. The crowd is turning ugly. I'm fed up with these celebrity authors. They treat their readers without any respect. We had a proper writer here a few years ago – Salman Rushdie – even with all that *fatwa* business. He was a joy.' Their conversation was cut short by a sudden cheer. Nick turned to see Steve Moran descend the last steps of a rather grand staircase with an exaggerated landing. 'Oh, here we go, Excuse me, sir.' Norman made his way to the desk to join Moran, who was acknowledging the crowd with a 'We are not worthy' bow. Nick joined the 'signing' queue.

Norman would pass Moran each book and then Steve would take over. 'There you go, Donna. Bless you.' He made brief eye contact with the first half dozen fans but then, robot-like, applied his signature to each open book without even looking up. Nick could see the sales assistants had written the names on Post-it notes stuck on the front of the books so Moran didn't have to raise his eyes – unless anyone merited a proper look. 'All right, Becky? Here you go, darling.'

'I love you, Steve.'

'And I love you too!' He gave the attractive young woman in front of him a wink and smirked at Norman, who remained busy passing over the books for him to sign. Nick was now second in the queue.

'There you go. Thanks, man.' Another fan was dispatched swiftly by Moran without raising his eyes.

Norman looked up to see Nick standing in front of the desk. 'I'm sorry, I can't seem to find your book, sir? Oh, It's you.'

'That's all right. I have my own copy. He knows my name. Hello, Steve, remember me?

Moran raised his head. 'Oh, shit.'

Norman had become slightly perplexed. 'You have to buy a book that Mr Moran can sign, sir.'

'No, I don't, Norman. I wrote the bloody thing. A fact the so-called author here failed to mention on *Midday Chat* in front of millions of viewers. All your own work, Steve? You begged me to invent your miserable life for you.'

'You must buy a book, sir.'

'Tell you what, Norman, I've got a cheque he can sign. How about that?'

Norman felt it was time to be more assertive. 'I'm afraid I must ask you to step aside, sir. '

Moran was getting irritated. 'Step aside? Is that the best you can do? Are you fucking serious, you berk?'

Nick was in his element now. 'And for all the work I did, you still haven't paid me my fee.'

'Well, what little you did was rubbish. Not worth a penny.'

'Bit late now. You were very happy when I was writing the book.'

Steve Moran turned to Norman. 'Don't they have proper security in this place? Quick!'

'What about that chapter I wrote about you training with the SAS, Steve? I wouldn't have thought you'd need any help.' Nick thought the confrontation was going quite well until a fan grabbed him by the shoulder. 'Come on, you tosser, you're holding us all up. Piss off.'

Moran nodded to his new ally. 'Exactly, mate. If you let me sell the books, I might be able to pay you. Now fuck off.' He stood up and gave Nick a hefty shove.

Nick regained his balance and, determined to at least go down with all guns blazing, decided to dish out what Charlie

Robertson would describe as 'a clump'. Unfortunately, Steve Moran ducked and didn't sink to the floor as Nick intended. 'Right, you wanker. 'You'll get nothing from me now.'

By now the shop was in uproar. Various sales assistants and customers were shouting and grabbing at Nick. Two security men arrived, put Nick in arm locks and dragged him towards the back of the store. Books and trestle tables were sent flying as the struggling Nick shouted to the shocked queue of Moran fans, 'I wrote it! Me! You should be asking for *my* signature!'

8

'He should be here by now.' Grace raised her hands in frustration. 'I'm sorry, Danesh.'

Danesh eyed the rucksack at his feet. 'Perhaps he does not want me here.'

Ben speed-dialled Nick's number. He was becoming more frustrated by his father's absence – he had promised to be home by eight. 'Don't worry, it'll be fine.'

Danesh smiled doubtfully. He was very grateful to Grace, of course, and now to Ben, but was entirely convinced this was not going to work out. Why should it? Nothing ever did for him.

Marcel looked up from his iPad, 'M . . . m . . . mum. I'm h . . . hungry.'

'Darling, I'll get you something in a minute.'

'Takeaw . . . way?' Marcel looked hopeful.

'Maybe. Just be patient.' Grace gave Marcel's arm a squeeze.

Ben shook his head. 'It's no good – can't get through to him.'

'Perhaps he's been taken ill,' suggested Grace.

'Taken drunk more like,' said Ben.

'Look, we're going to have to go. Marcel needs some food.'

'Tell you what, Danesh' – Ben was too embarrassed to let

Danesh leave without something coming out of the visit – 'I'll show you your room.'

After Grace and Marcel had left, Ben walked Danesh around the flat with as much enthusiasm as he could muster, and guided him to a tiny box room. 'You go first, as there isn't really much room for two.' Paperwork, folders and numerous newspaper and Internet cuttings littered the floor. The single bed was covered with items of clothing. 'Sorry, we meant to tidy up.'

'Nothing compared to what happens after the Morality Police have ransacked your home.'

'Why did you have to leave, Danesh?'

'I upset the government on social media. They don't like anyone who disagrees with the regime.'

Ben was at a loss. 'You could stay tonight if you want. We could sort your room out.'

'What will your father say?'

'He'll be fine. He likes to make a fuss about things, but he'll agree with me . . . and Grace. For all his faults, he's usually quite reliable.'

Danesh raised his eyebrows. 'I do not know what they are. My father was executed when I was a baby.'

'Oh, I'm sorry, I—'

'That's OK. I have never known anything different.'

'What about your mother?'

'She is still in Iran with my brothers and sisters. They are in danger.'

'Will they be able to join you?'

Danesh smiled weakly. 'I don't know. That is up to the Home Office and . . . Grace.'

'I'm sure she'll do her best for you.'

Danesh nodded. 'She is. I could have nobody better helping me. And you and your father.'

Ben was silent for a moment. 'My dad can be difficult, but he's all right really.'

Nick got home to discover a complete stranger on the sofa watching *Reservoir Dogs*.

He was not in the best of moods. In retrospect he had not got his evening in the custody suite at Charing Cross police station off to the best start by accusing the officers who'd brought him in of running a police state and being basically fascists, or by banging on the custody sergeant's desk to emphasise the point. It had then taken several hours to bring them round from charging him with criminal damage or threatening behaviour to his contention that it was all 'just a few books on the floor – and only one title'. '*I am not a man of violence*,' he had concluded with the thunderous piety of Martin Luther King. Eventually he had persuaded Sergeant Finchley that he wasn't a risk to the general public and would not abscond, and been released on the understanding that he would not go anywhere near Steve Moran.

The young man stood up. 'Good evening, Mr Greenwood. I am Danesh.'

'Ah. Of course. Yes – look, I'm so sorry. I was detained. Literally.'

'You are very kind.'

'Well, I haven't exactly agreed to – where's Ben?'

'In the shower. You have a very nice bathroom.'

'Hi Dad, thanks for turning up.' An irritated Ben, wrapped in a bath towel, glared at his father. 'This is Danesh.'

Danesh offered a hand and with the other grabbed the remote and paused Mr Orange just as he was about to shoot someone.

'I said he could stay—'

'But I didn't—'

'It's sorted.'

'Ben, can you come with me into the kitchen?'

Nick closed the door behind them. 'Ben,' he whispered, 'I said we had to meet him first.'

'You weren't here. I had to make an executive decision.'

'"Executive decision"? This isn't the United Nations.'

'You should hear his story, Dad. It's really gutting. This is the least we can do. He's literally sitting next door with a sense of hopelessness about life.'

'*Reservoir Dogs* will do that.'

'You hold his future in the palm of your hand.'

'Ben, this is not helping.'

'You have the power to help him start a new life.'

'Enough!' Nick sighed. 'What does Grace say?'

'She doesn't know yet. You wouldn't want to disappoint her, would you, Dad?'

'No – what do you mean?'

Ben opened the door. 'Danesh, you're in.'

*

'Is that the best you could do, Sam? Flowers from a petrol station?' Kitty flung what could only loosely be described as 'a bouquet' to the end of her bed. 'You're very late.'

'I said I'd be here by eleven thirty.'

'It's now ten past six.'

'Kitty, you're wearing your watch upside down.'

Kitty gazed at it. 'I thought time was dragging.'

'How long are you going to be here?'

'Another week or so. They are trying to get me walking, but it's far too early. I keep telling them about my arthritic knees, but they don't seem to listen.'

'And who are *they*?

'The physiotherapists. And all because of that *buffoon* you introduced me to.'

'He feels very guilty about it,' said Sam.

'So he should. He attempted to make amends by sending me what he's written so far. There's one page where it says I've had my leg broken by someone called Roy Keane. Who is *Roy Keane*?'

'I think that must be from one of Nick's previous books.'

'This has turned into a farce. And I've never done farce. Edie says I should find someone else.'

Sam was about to mention Kitty's ill-fated run in a production of *Trousers Off* at the Whitehall when a physiotherapist, complete with walking frame over her shoulder, bustled to the bedside. Kitty raised her eyes heavenward. 'Not you again.'

'The nurses should have got you into a chair.'

'They tried.'

The physio plonked the frame down beside Kitty's bed. 'Not hard enough. Come on, pet, let's be having you.'

'I am not your pet.'

'Up we go.'

'Mischief, thou art afoot!' wailed Kitty as her tormentor eased her to her feet. 'Take thou what course thou wilt!'

Nick had taken refuge in a Starbucks before his next therapy session, for which he was an hour early. He had experienced timing issues over the years with his various therapists. When late for a session he had been accused of being 'resistant', when early of being 'neurotic', and once, when actually on the dot, 'obsessive'. As he tucked into his blueberry muffin and double espresso he thought he would make use of the time by writing up his latest interview with Kitty. He was soon distracted by two men at the next table discussing whether robots and the use of Artificial Intelligence might be a threat to their employment as estate agents. Nick thought it was only a matter of time.

He soon realised that as ever a public space was too distracting to work in, and set about some old Wordle puzzles, becoming particularly annoyed at *snafu*, which he thought unfairly American. He'd always tried to second-guess the solutions by choosing US alternatives when British answers seemed much more apt, but this was going too far. His mobile phone rang. 'Hi, is that Nick Greenwood?'

'Yes, who's speaking?'

'My name is Elysha Hourglass. I'm calling about a book.'

'Which book?'

'My book.'

'How did you get my number?' Nick also wondered where she got that name.

'From your agent, Clarissa.'

'Clarissa? She's not actually – never mind.'

'I want to write a book, and you've been recommended as someone who could help.'

'Well, that's always nice.' Nick was always a slave to flattery. 'Who recommended me?'

'A friend of mine,' Elysha continued hurriedly. 'The thing is, would you be able to help?'

'I don't know. It depends on how much work. I've got quite a few things on at the moment.'

Elysha sighed. 'Look, Mr Greenwood, I can pay up front. And I know you don't come cheap. So I'm prepared to part with some serious money.'

Nick was immediately interested. He couldn't imagine where the 'don't come cheap' line came from, but he wasn't going to ask now. 'Well, I suppose I could squeeze you in . . . I'll call you to make a time to meet.'

'Thanks very much, Mr Greenwood. Don't leave it too long. I've actually written half a dozen chapters.'

'Can you give me a clue about what you do?'

'I'm a glamour model. That's all I want to tell you at this stage.'

Well, this was something new. 'Email them to me. You'll need my email address.'

'I've got that.'

How did she know his email address? Never mind, he was

impressed by her politeness and deference, but even more by the prospect of serious money.

The therapy session began with Steve Moran. An unrepentant Nick had laid down his marker. 'This isn't going to end here.'

'And what do you mean by that?' Deirdre was genuinely intrigued.

As Nick related the events of the previous evening Deirdre shifted uneasily in her chair. 'You need to be careful, Nick. We've never discussed your need for some anger management guidance.'

'Oh, I will. I'm not daft.' Nick thought she might have noticed this before.

'You can't afford to get arrested.'

'I can't afford anything much at the moment. Including you.'

'Be careful. These things can escalate. What else is on your mind?'

'Grace. My neighbour.'

'OK...'

There was a silence before Nick continued. 'We've been spending more time together recently and – well, I think I like her.'

Deirdre put down her pad and paper. 'How much?'

'I think I *really* like her.'

'Have you told her?'

'Of course not. It's much too early.'

'Do you think she likes you?'

'Difficult to say. But yes, in a sort of way.'

'What sort of way?'

'Well, not romantically. I don't think. Why would she want to get involved with me? I'm ten years older than her. Not in the best of health and not much money. Otherwise I'm the perfect catch.'

'Have you lost confidence in yourself?'

'I don't want to spoil our friendship. And it's very awkward, her living upstairs. I *would* like to move on now.'

Deirdre furrowed her brow. 'I realise we haven't talked about your illness – I'm interested that you've avoided it.'

'I'm seeing the consultant later on today.'

'Doesn't the future scare you just a little?'

'Of course. I'm not looking forward to any treatment.'

'I wasn't talking about the treatment. Do you recall in our last session, we touched upon the subject of your mortality?'

'You asked me how I would feel if the treatment didn't work.'

'And you replied, "Dead."'

'Well, it was a bit of daft question, Deirdre.'

'You chose a glib answer, which is not unlike you.'

Nick pretended to appear perplexed. 'Isn't it?'

Deirdre gave him an old-fashioned look. 'Anyway.' She paused for effect. 'I think we should explore it a little further today.'

'Well, course I worry about Ben if something happened to me. Although he and Danesh seem to be getting on well—'

'Who is Danesh?'

'An asylum seeker. He's living with us temporarily.'

'You haven't told me about him.'

'I'm doing it as a favour to Grace.'

'I see.' Deirdre raised her eyebrows. 'We're back to Grace.'

Nick had to admit he was enjoying having Danesh in the flat. Because he wasn't allowed to work, Danesh had been very helpful around the house, and dispelled any lingering doubts Nick might have had that he was a threat to national security. Anyone who knocked up a pretty good shepherd's pie, gleaned from watching daytime cookery programmes, couldn't possibly be a terrorist.

'I also wanted to talk about Amy. I've been thinking about her a lot since our last session. About her illness and how she died. I've even been dreaming about her.'

Deirdre sighed. 'Nick, why did you wait until the end of the session to talk about this?'

'I don't know. Avoidance, I suppose. And guilt about what happened to her.'

'Guilt? Why?'

'Maybe if I had agreed to have her back, she might not have had the stroke and ended up like she did.'

'You don't know that.'

'I'm not sure about anything any more.'

'This is so important, Nick, but I'm sorry, we'll have to pick this up another time. It's just that—'

'I know. My time's up. Rather like Amy's was.'

Dr Hanson shuffled in her seat and twirled her stethoscope in the time-honoured fashion. 'I'm afraid the biopsy confirmed that you do have prostate cancer.'

Though Nick had known this was probably the case, it still came as a shock. He looked to Dr Hanson for more.

'But the good news is we think we've caught it early.'

'Ah. Well, I suppose that would be good news.' Nick sighed deeply.

'But we do need to see how far the disease has progressed. We'll arrange a scan as soon as possible.'

'What's your gut feeling, Dr Hanson?'

'I'm afraid I'm not a gastroenterologist.' Now Dr Hanson was doing the jokes. 'I'll book you in to the clinic to have your catheter removed – the swelling should have gone down by now.'

'Thanks, I think.'

'And in the meantime we'll put you on some medication that suppresses the testosterone in your body.'

'What sort of medication?'

'Hormones. Tablets and three-monthly injections.'

'Oh. I see. This is all a bit of a shock.'

'Of course. You'll need some time for this to sink in. Do you have any family, Mr Greenwood?'

'My son – he's twenty-one. I don't know how I'll be able to tell him.'

'I can give you some information and contact details for support groups.' Dr Hanson handed him a sheaf of leaflets. 'Do you have any questions for now?'

'Nothing I can think of at the moment. I can always look up things on the Internet.'

Dr Hanson frowned. 'I wouldn't do that, Mr Greenwood. You might find all sorts of things that you really don't want to read. There's a lot of misinformation out there. Please call me instead.' She smiled at Nick.

As Nick trudged down the hospital escalator reality hit him. Surely this couldn't be it? He had so much to live for, hadn't he? Should he make a bucket list? He started to feel breathless, his legs began to wobble, and so he sat down on a bench outside the main entrance. He really wasn't ready to die.

He wished had hadn't fallen out with his best school friend, James, about a girl. He wondered what Clare was doing now. He might google her later.

And there was that unfortunate remark about Rooster Cogburn he'd made years ago to an old man wearing an eye patch.

He never had written that Booker Prize-winning novel or learnt to play the piano.

Had he done enough for Ben? What about his father?

He thought about his baby brother.

And how would he look, thin and emaciated? He hoped he wouldn't lose his hair during the treatment. And what sort of pain might he have to endure? Would he now have to wear one of those little-man lapel badges the veteran Sky football pundits always sported?

After a third customer and two waiters had asked for selfies with Junior, Clarissa had told the manageress of the Hungry Horse to prevent the couple being approached.

Junior shrugged. 'All part of the job, babe. Cool place, tho'? Voted number-one restaurant in Soho.'

'Number one in prices.' Clarissa pointed at the contents of the menu. 'Forty-two pounds for lamb chops! Truffle and champagne humble pie a mere twenty-five pounds! Humble?'

'Good job you're a vegetarian. Hey, don't worry, Clar, if the book keeps selling we can afford plenty of lunches ... dinners ... and breakfasts. You get me?'

Clarissa smiled weakly. 'I think you'll find you'll have made a lot more money from football than you will from royalties.'

'Even better.' Junior squeezed Clarissa's hand rather too tightly for her liking. 'There's something I've been meaning to say to you.' He clasped both her hands. 'I'd like you to meet my mum.'

'Oh, would you?' Clarissa unclasped.

'She's just gone back to Grenada. That's where she's from. We could have a holiday there. It's beautiful, man. Extinct volcanos, breathtaking mountains, forests of teak and mahogany, crystal-clear streams, palm trees swaying on sun-kissed beaches, and delicious spices that—'

'You obviously love it.'

'I've been reading the brochures.'

'It sounds divine.'

'And then who knows what could happen?'

'What? What could happen?'

'Well, it's a very romantic place.'

'Is that what the brochure says?'

'No, that's me talking.'

'Well, if your work as football punter ends—'

'*Pundit.*'

'Whatever. Anyway, you could always get a job at the Grenada tourist board.'

'The thing is, Clarissa, I like you. I do like you.'

'Yes, we work very well together. In bed it certainly works.'

'I wasn't thinking of the work. Or the sex, which is great. It's you and me. We're good together.'

'Mmm ... yes.' Clarissa gazed desperately around the restaurant for another selfie-seeker to come to her rescue. The manageress was doing her job only too well.

'I've had a lot of girlfriends, but there's never been anyone like you.'

'I can see you've been staring at us for a while,' said Clarissa to a lone diner at the next table. 'I expect you want a photograph of Junior? Don't be shy.' Before the startled diner could respond Clarissa had jumped out of her seat, grabbed his mobile and snapped the even more surprised Junior. She beckoned the manageress. 'We've changed our minds. Anyone who wants to take a selfie is welcome.'

Nick had decided to walk home from the hospital to try and get his head around the diagnosis. Along the way he tried to call a few people. It was unlike him, but he felt he needed to share the news. Grace was the first person he wanted to talk to speak to, but she was in the middle of a client consultation. He left a message for Sam, who annoyingly never left his phone on. Ringing his dad was out of the question – he didn't want to worry the old man who, in his utter discomfort, would probably only start singing 'Every Time We Say Goodbye'. He even got as far as dialling Frankie's number, before realising how desperate he must have got. It was like calling Piers Morgan for a counselling session. He was dreading telling Ben, and thought about ringing or even texting him — but that would be cowardly and, let's face it, his son's previous attempts to comfort him had been somewhat disastrous. He'd wait until he got home and explain to him face to face what was happening. He wanted to remain upbeat for his son's sake, but Ben was surprisingly perceptive.

Nick opened the door of his flat with some trepidation, but was saved from any immediate confession by the sound of Marcel, who was inevitably playing FIFA with Ben. He was about to enter the living room when he heard the two of them in deep conversation. And it wasn't about football.

'C . . . c . . . can I ask you a qu . . . question, Ben?'

'That goal wasn't your fault, it was my brilliance.' Ben patted his opponent on the shoulder.

'It's not about FIFA.' Marcel rested his controller on the sofa.

Ben smiled. 'I'm sure Junior will get you the Spurs shirt.'

Marcel shook his head. 'It's something else. Some . . . thing s . . . s . . . ser . . . serious. Completely.'

'Oh. OK.' Ben gave Marcel his full attention.

'Why have I got Downssyndrome?' Marcel ran the two words into one.

'Ah.' Ben obviously hadn't been expecting this. The subject had never been discussed before.

'I don't know. I think it's complicated.'

Marcel frowned. 'Why?'

Ben was floundering. 'Um, well, something to do with chromosomes.'

'I don't know what they are.'

Ben wasn't exactly sure himself. 'Haven't you asked your mum about this?'

'Yes. She just says she loves me as I am. M ... more than anyone.'

'Of course she does.'

'But it isn't fair that I've got Downssyndrome. I don't want to have it. I want to be independent.'

'But what about your friends?'

'I like Max.'

'There you are.'

'But he's got Downssyndrome too. I want lots of friends without Downssyndrome.'

'I'm your friend, Marcel.'

'I want to go out on my own.'

'Well, you don't need lots of friends to go out on your own.'

'I want to do both, dickhead.' Marcel chuckled.

'Hey, that's a bit cheeky.' Ben gave the boy a playful punch. But he did feel a bit of a dickhead.

'It isn't fair. I can't do things. I can't run fast, or ride a bike very well.'

'Yes, but you always try your best. That's the main thing.'

'And I want a dad.'

'Well, I'm not sure ...'

'And a girlfriend.'

'Look, I'm twenty-one and I haven't got a girlfriend. And I don't have Down's syndrome.'

'That's because you can be a dickhead.' Marcel laughed even louder.

Ben was becoming more uncomfortable. 'Come on, Marcel. Let's carry on. I think my goal was offside.'

Nick decided this was the moment to intervene. He went back to the front door, made a lot of noise and entered the sitting room. 'Hi, you two. Everything OK?'

'Yes, we were just playing and talking,' said Ben.

Marcel raised a finger to his lips. 'Sshh, Ben.'

Ben nodded over-enthusiastically. 'Yup. We're fine.'

Nick hovered. 'Eaten?'

'Yup.'

Marcel waved an empty Domino's box at Nick.

Nick smiled. 'Your favourite? Margherita?'

The usually ebullient Marcel didn't answer, but stared at the television screen. Nick's questions were met with a shrug. That was the thing about Marcel. There was never any pretence about his mood or how he felt. You knew where you stood with him. Nick made a mental note to report back to Grace, although he was certain this wouldn't be a new conversation between mother and son.

When Marcel had gone home, Nick suggested he and Ben share a beer together. 'Yes, please, Dad.'

Nick opened a couple of bottles of Broadside. 'Cheers, Ben.'

'Cheers, Dad.' They clinked bottles.

'Ben, there's something I need to tell you. I saw the doctor today . . . Well . . . she confirmed that I have prostate cancer. But she said it was very common in men of my age and there was no need to worry. They caught it early.' Nick took a large swig.

'But you'll be all right?'

'Yes, you don't have to think about letting out my room just yet.'

'Dad, I didn't really mean all that stuff. I was worried. Especially after what happened to Mum.'

'I'm sorry. I'm sure I could have handled it all much better.'

'That's OK, Dad.' Ben cupped the bottle in his hands without drinking.

'The doctor said I need a scan to make sure it hasn't spread.'

'What? I thought you said you'd caught it early.'

'I did. Just precautionary. I'm sure it will be fine.'

'Yeah.' After a pause Ben glanced at his father. 'It had better be. I'm not sure how I could manage without you.'

Nick squeezed his son's hand. Father and son gazed affectionately at each other until the silence became unbearable and Ben had to look away. 'I'm glad you told me.'

'Me too.'

9

'Kitty, I feel awful about all this.'

Kitty Lawrence struck Nick on his knee with her walking stick. 'So you should. Look at me! I can hardly move.'

'I'm very grateful you've agreed to continue with the book.'

'You can thank Sam for that. He convinced me to give you a second chance.'

'And it's great that you have your own room. We can work in private.'

'Oh, I demanded peace and quiet. I told them I didn't want fans clamouring for autographs and delaying my recovery.'

Nick couldn't imagine Kitty being mobbed by fans fighting their way to the orthopaedic ward. 'Are you comfortable? Then perhaps we can begin?'

'You sound like an episode of *Listen with Mother*.'

'No, I was genuinely—'

'I did do a couple of episodes of *Jackanory*, as it happens. A young whippersnapper of a director dared to ask me what I'd done. I emulated Dame Edith Evans and replied, "Do you mean this morning?"'

Nick laughed. 'I bet he was more careful after that.'

'Oh, I didn't leave it there. I went on to tell him that Kenneth Tynan wrote that I was the definitive Viola in *Twelfth Night* and the most assured Saint Joan since Sybil Thorndike. I think that was Tynan too.'

'It was Tynan.'

'Terrible man. But sometimes absolutely correct in his criticism. There was one actor who was so over-the top he wrote, "Not content to have the audience in the palm of his hand, he goes one further and clenches his fist." I can't recall who . . . it could have been so many.' Kitty stared into the distance. 'Where was I before you interrupted me?'

Nick glanced at his laptop. 'Wilfred Hyde White.'

'Oh, yes. He was doing a matinee in Worthing.'

'Yes, I've got that, Kitty. I'd like to ask you about your time in Hollywood.'

'It's not a time I like talk about. You'll have to do some research, and I'll fill in the details. That's your job, isn't it?'

'It's better if you give me something to work on.'

'I think I told you in our first meeting. I couldn't bear the place. So vulgar. All that false enthusiasm . . . it all meant nothing. Do you know, superficiality is one thing I can't bear. One day you are going to be the next Katherine Hepburn, the next they don't want to know you. It wasn't for me.'

Nick nodded eagerly. 'Someone once described Hollywood as Picasso's bathroom.'

'I've no idea what that means, but I'm sure I agree with them.'

'But Kitty, we must include that period in the book.'

'Perhaps. My agent thought it would be wise for me to make the move if I wanted to be a worldwide star. How wrong he was.'

'Can you tell me about the films you did?'

'First I had done a small part for MGM, filmed here in Borehamwood: *The VIPs*, some time in the Sixties – you'll have to look up the date. All-star cast: Richard Burton, Liz Taylor, Orson Welles, Louis Jourdan – oh, he was so handsome – Maggie Smith, Margaret Rutherford . . .'

'What about behind the scenes?' Nick's hands were poised over his laptop.

'Oh, I didn't see much of them. Although Liz Taylor was in the middle of a torrid love affair with Burton. She was very grand – she demanded that two walls of her dressing room were knocked down to make a three-room suite, which included a queen-sized bed. I suppose that was for Mr Burton.' Kitty gave out a surprisingly saucy giggle. 'Margaret Rutherford's only request was a Baby Belling stove, which she used for a fry-up every night with her husband Stringer. She managed to get him in every film she was in. Gay, you know. Hopeless actor. Dear old Margaret. You should write her biography, you know.'

'I think it's been done.'

'I was then lured to Hollywood to be in a Hitchcock film. He barely spoke to me. So obsessed with that Grace Kelly. Although I have to say, Cary Grant was very handsome. Then they cast me in a Western opposite John Wayne. I can't recall the title.' Kitty looked at Nick for help.

'That would be . . . *The Revenge of Jake Kincaid*.'

'Oh dear, yes. I was kidnapped by some Indians, and John Wayne was my uncle who rescued me. Personally, I would rather have remained with the Apaches. Finally, I got "gang-banged" – I think that's the expression – by a group of motorcyclists in a film called *Angels from Fresno*. That was not why I went to RADA. That was the final straw. I never told Ernest about the film. He would have been appalled. Luckily it was never released in the UK.'

'Was there any fall-out from it?'

'I sacked my agent.'

'And that was it for you in Hollywood?'

'Oh, they begged me to stay and made all kinds of extravagant offers. They even promised me a romantic comedy with Robert Redford. But I came home. I think that will do for now.'

'I just want to ask you about this, Kitty.' Nick produced the postcard of the group of soldiers signed by 'Hubby'. 'Who is he?'

'Why do you ask?'

'Because I found another photograph of the same man marked in green ink on the postcard. At least, I think it's the same man, but he looks much older and thinner. Here – look.' Nick handed Kitty a photograph of a soldier in jodhpurs, button-down tunic, service cap and carrying a swagger stick. His smiley, carefree expression had disappeared, replaced by a haunted, vacuous look.

'It is the same man, Nick.'

'I just wondered if you knew what happened to him.'

'Of course I do. He's my grandfather.'

'It's just that—'

'This isn't for the book. I'm sorry but I'm very tired. Please go. I have to go back to bed now. My hip is extremely painful.'

Nick stood up. 'Perhaps I can help?'

'I don't think so. I don't want my other hip fractured.'

As Nick approached the nurse's station, his mobile rang. Charlie Robertson's moon face took up most of the screen.

'Blimey, that's a bit close, Charlie. Wouldn't a normal phone call work?'

'I wanted to see your face – I can always tell if someone is lying.'

'About what?'

'About Ashley.'

'Oh.' Despite the generous offer Nick had done virtually nothing about finding Charlie's daughter.

'How are you are getting on?'

'Oh, well, getting closer.'

'You just scratched your nose.'

'What?'

'I've played enough poker to know that's a "tell".'

'No, just a bit of hay fever.'

'In March?'

'Anyhow, I've got . . . I've got . . .'

'Feelers out?'

'Yes! That's it.' Nick resisted a tremendous urge to scratch his nose.

'Good. That's what I like to hear. You'll be in touch when you have some news, then.'

'Of course. But I still don't know why you don't use those goons.'

'They're a bit busy.'

'With what?'

'Well, you might be interested to know they'll be having a word with Steve Moran soon.'

'What kind of word?'

'Just a little advice.'

'Charlie, I really don't want any trouble. I've already had a brush with the law.'

'You? A brush with the law? That's priceless.'

'Will you please get me a nurse?' Kitty called out. 'I need to rest.'

'Look, Charlie, I've got to go.' Nick turned his mobile so Charlie could see an increasingly impatient Kitty attempting to get back into bed. 'I've got an old lady in trouble.'

Charlie cackled noisily. 'I wouldn't say that too loudly, Nicky boy!'

A few days later Nick found himself back at the police station, his presence having been requested by WPC Mackenzie. Worried about what was to follow, he was ready to play the cancer card if necessary – indeed, exaggerate his condition depending on the severity of the charges. If it was 'common assault', he'd say he'd only just been diagnosed and was in a state of anxiety. 'Actual bodily harm' would mean his life was limited, and if charged with 'grievous bodily harm', the most worrying outcome, Nick would tell WPC Mackenzie he had just weeks to live.

In fact, WPC Mackenzie greeted him cheerfully in the waiting room. 'Some good news for you. We aren't going to take this further. We spoke to Mr Moran. It appears he isn't going to press charges. He doesn't want the publicity.'

'That's a first. He's usually happy to open a fridge.'

'But you must stay away from Mr Moran. All right?'

'I don't want to go anywhere near him.'

'Next time you might not be so fortunate. Not only could you have been charged with actual bodily harm, but this could also have been a breach of the peace. Luckily for you Scrimshaws don't want to pursue the matter.'

Nick breathed out. 'I understand.'

'Just before you go . . . What's he like? I've never met anyone off the telly.'

'Steve Moran? You're asking the wrong person. I have worked with other celebrities.'

'Go on.' WPC Mackenzie sat forward in expectation.

'Junior Hamilton . . . Frankie Morrison . . . Kitty Lawrence . . . Charlie Robertson . . .'

WPC Mackenzie looked blank. After a while she said, 'The name Charlie Robertson rings a bell . . .'

'Siren, more like.' Nick bade the policewoman goodbye and was on his way. A free man!

He was, of course, fooling himself, because outside the police station a black SUV screeched to a halt and Bogdan Dumitrescu jumped out and grabbed Nick by the shoulders. 'Inside, please, Mr Greenwood.'

'Oh, not again! What is it now?'

'We tell you in the car.'

'Mind my head!'

'We have been on health-and-safety course.'

Leon King turned around. 'We're taking you home, Nick.'

'Well, that's a relief. Leon, why the taxi service?'

'The guvnor wanted to know what you were doing at the cop shop.'

'How did you know about that? They were asking me about my altercation with Steve Moran at the bookshop. It's OK, they aren't going to press charges.'

Nick's new ringtone of Stevie Wonder's 'Sir Duke' rang. It was Frankie.

'I'm willing to go down to fifty grand?'

'Frankie, could we just drop the subject?'

Leon was overtaking a cyclist who was annoying him on the wrong side of the road, causing an approaching car to swerve around a stationary bus.

Nick dived the length of the back seat, only daring to lift himself up when the cacophony of hooting had ceased. 'Leon, for goodness' sake! We could have all been killed!'

'Would you like us to see to him?' said Bogdan.

'Who? No! I don't want you to go anywhere near Steve Moran! Do you understand me? I mean it, both of you. I don't want anything to happen to him.'

Danesh had just settled down in front of the television for the afternoon with a bag of Haribo Tangfastics and a re-run of *Midsummer Murders* when the doorbell went. Standing in the doorway was one of the most beautiful English women he had ever seen. 'Hello, is Nick here?'

Danesh could barely speak. 'No . . . no . . . no. He's out.'

'Do you know when he'll be back?' The girl gave him a look that cut him in half.

'No, sorry.'

'OK. I'll give him a bell.'

Danesh had no idea why she would give him a bell when the one on the front door one worked perfectly well, but decided not to ask. 'No, please come in. You are his girlfriend?'

The young woman laughed. 'You kidding? No, he's helping me with my book.'

'He should be back soon. He's seeing his therapist.'

'Blimey! Sending him round the twist already, am I?'

Danesh had no idea what this meant either, but he would forgive this woman anything. 'Come in, have a cup of tea.'

'Cup of tea would be lovely.' Elysha kicked off her shoes and threw off her coat, revealing torn jeans and a dazzling turquoise mohair sweater two sizes too big.

From the kitchen Danesh called out, 'What do you do?'

'I'm what you call a glamour model.'

Danesh stepped back into the sitting room. 'A model. That is very good.'

'You think so? Not everybody does. How about you?'

'I want to be a doctor. Grace from upstairs is helping me. You know Grace?'

'No.'

'She is amazing. I hope to stay in this country. I cannot return home.'

Ben, hearing the conversation in the next room, came to investigate, and found Danesh in deep conversation with a stunning young woman.

'This is Elysha.'

'Oh. Hi. I'm Ben.'

'He is Nick's son.'

'I've come to see your dad.'

'*Really?*' Ben stared at Elysha. Why would this wondrous woman possibly want to see his father?

'About a book.'

Ben sat down on the sofa next to Elysha while Danesh straddled the sofa waiting for the kettle to boil. 'You're working on a book with Dad?'

'Sort of. I gave him some chapters to read.'

Ben made himself comfortable on the sofa and called out, 'I'll have one too, Danesh.'

'I've only spoken to him on the phone. So I wanted to see him face to face.'

Ben stared at Elysha lost for words and a little annoyed with himself at being so dumbstruck. But then he had never set eyes on anyone quite so gorgeous in real life – and so natural. He was disappointed in himself that he was so taken in by her looks. This was 'the male gaze' he had always railed against at its most atavistic. But he couldn't stop gazing at her.

'You have two jobs? A writer as well as a model?' Danesh had returned with a hurriedly made cup of tea.

Elysha laughed. 'If only. Trying to be a writer. I pose on a couple of TV channels. Hot Babe and Even Hotter Babes. Not completely naked. Lingerie and bikinis. In super HD.' Elysha smiled coyly at each man in turn.

Ben was in a terrible dilemma. He should have been appalled at how she had been exploited by the patriarchal society, the objectification of the female form and the sexualizing of women that had led her to such employment. But she was ... *breathtaking*! And it was her body to show off, wasn't it? He looked to Danesh for guidance. There came none. Danesh seemed unaware of his predicament.

'What is a hot babe?' Danesh looked genuinely puzzled.

Elysha gave Ben a knowing look. 'Perhaps you should ask Ben.'

Ben blushed. 'Oh ... I wouldn't say ... I couldn't ... have you finished the book, Elysha?'

'I've written six chapters. I've got the rest in my head, if you know what I mean.'

Danesh nodded wisely. 'You must be very clever.'

'We'll see what Nick says. Anyway, I'd better go.' Elysha took a final sip from her mug and got up.

'I'm sure Dad will be back soon. Would you like another cup?'

'No, I just called on the off chance. Tell him to get in touch.'

'Defo.' Ben had never used this word before and immediately regretted it.

Danesh jumped to his feet. 'I will show you out.'

What had made Ben say '*Defo*'? Marcel was right – he *was* a dickhead. He'd been reduced to a blubbering wreck by Elysha's looks – the very thing that was not supposed to matter. Life would have been much easier if he was sexist, lookist and entirely apolitical, but he had to be true to himself – but what was that in such circumstances? In any case, he didn't stand much of a chance. With his dark, curly hair, open face and deep-set green eyes Ben wasn't a bad-looking boy, although he was a little conscious of his slightly fleshy nose, for which he naturally blamed his dad. But the muscular, lithe Danesh was in a different league. A couple of inches taller than Ben, stunningly handsome, and with eyelashes that could extinguish a candle. These thoughts were still going around Ben's head when Danesh eventually returned, looking rather pleased with himself.

'You took your time saying goodbye.'

Danesh shrugged his shoulders as he sat down next to Ben. 'Very nice girl. Very beautiful too.'

'Yes, she is . . . I mean – she seemed very nice.'

'Beautiful inside and outside.' Danesh beamed at Ben.

'You think so. You can't know her very well. You just met.'

'I am a good judge of people. That is something I have learned.'

'Do you approve of what she does?'

'I neither approve nor criticise – but I respect her. I try to adapt to Western ways. Some I approve, some I do not.'

'But doesn't Islamic law . . . ?'

'You assume that I am a Muslim?'

'Well, I thought . . .'

'I have no religion.'

'Oh.' Ben was cross with himself for lazy stereotyping.

'I respect her so much. I will respect her again when I see her tomorrow.'

Junior had rung Nick while he was at the hospital. The timing was somewhat unfortunate as he was about to have his catheter removed. Junior's response of 'I'd better take you off loudspeaker' was hardly comforting.

Nick explained that they had to check he could pee without the catheter, and if he couldn't another one would have to be inserted.

'*Ow*, man!' Junior guffawed. 'I don't like the sound of that. Can't be good for your sex life.'

'I don't have a sex life.'

'What about that woman who lives above you? Marcel's mum. I thought you had a thing going?'

'I do not have a thing going with Grace! Are you sure we're off loudspeaker?'

Junior explained that he was outside Nick's building and had brought the shirt for Marcel.

'Ring Grace's bell,' Nick said. 'Marcel should be home from school. He'll be thrilled to meet you.'

Grace was at the door when Junior had climbed the stairs. 'Marcel', she called out, 'I've got a surprise for you.'

Marcel rushed in from his bedroom. He liked surprises. 'J . . . J . . . Junior! You're famous!' Marcel extended his hand for a fist bump. 'Nice to meet you.'

'I've heard a lot about you, Marcel.'

'You know my name!'

Junior smiled at Marcel and handed him the shirt. 'Here you are. I got it signed by all the players for you.'

'That's ammm ... *azing*!' Marcel held the shirt against his body.

Grace ruffled her son's hair. 'What do you say, Marcel?'

'Thanks, Junior.'

'Don't you want to put it on?'

'Yes, Mum.' Marcel ran back into his bedroom clutching it.

So this was the woman Nick had mentioned on occasions? What had kept him from making a move? 'You're Grace? I've heard a lot about you.' Even Junior had noticed how patient Nick had been with him when they'd been working on the book. Perhaps he could do him a good turn? 'Nick's crazy about you.'

Grace raised her eyebrows. 'What are you talking about?'

'I reckon he's in love. You're all he talks about.'

'Don't be ridiculous.'

'He's shy – you know how some white folks are. You need to make a move on him.'

Grace shook her head in astonishment. 'I don't have a clue what you—'

Marcel returned wearing the shirt. On the back was emblazoned *Marcel 1*. He ran to Junior and gave him a hug. 'This is c-cool. I love it!' He burst into tears. 'I'm so happy.'

Junior gave Marcel a bear-like hug. 'You'll set me off! Look, maybe we could take in a game at Spurs, bro?'

'Amazing!' Marcel wiped his face and looked up at Junior. 'That would be c ... c ... cool.'

Junior gave Grace a knowing smile and the 'watching you' sign.

The following week proved particularly frustrating for Nick. He had attempted to chase Frankie with no discernible results, and was getting nowhere in locating Ashley Robertson. He had even sought advice from his son. 'You're roughly the same age – haven't you got any ideas where she might go during the day?'

'How would I know, Dad? Her dad's a gangster and he's hired you to find her? You'd better be careful.'

Nick considered returning the 'advance' Charlie had paid him, but Kitty hadn't paid him any of his fee, which wasn't surprising in the circumstances, so he could really use the money. He had reluctantly agreed to Kitty's immodest determination to entitle the book *A Grand Dame of the Theatre*, which she was sure would impel the government to take appropriate action in a future honours list. And to his intrigue and delight Grace had invited herself to dinner that evening.

More worrying still was the MRI scan. He stood looking warily at the glistening white torture chamber as the radiographer, a cool, attractive woman in her late forties, introduced herself. 'I am Ursula, and before you ask – the patients always do – I'm from Dresden, East Germany. You've had your catheter removed?'

'Indeed I have. That was a bundle of fun.'

'And you're passing water OK?'

'It's like Niagara Falls some nights.'

Ursula grimaced. 'Let me explain. The scanner uses radio

waves in a very strong magnetic field to create detailed pictures of the internal organs.'

'Can it pick up Radio 4?'

Ursula ignored this.

'Blame it on my nerves.'

'No dentures?'

Nick was a little aggrieved. 'No!'

'No metal pins or plates?' She studied his groin suspiciously.

'Definitely not.'

'No piercings?'

'Absolutely not.'

'Gunshot or shrapnel injuries?'

'I'm a pacifist. Although I did play Call of Duty once with my son.'

'The metal could be pulled out by powerful magnets in the machine. You might even explode. Yes? It will damage the expensive equipment.' She paused for dramatic affect. 'Big time.'

Nick eyed the scanner in some terror. 'I should mention, I do get claustrophobic.'

'You should be under there for less than half an hour. It may help if you close your eyes. Press this panic button if you need to contact us – we are on the other side of the glass.' Ursula placed a plastic 'bulb' attached to a lead on his lap. 'The machine can be very noisy at certain intervals. Do you want headphones with music?'

'I wouldn't mind something classical. No Schoenberg or Harrison Birtwistle...'

'I'm afraid you'll have to take your chances.' Ursula placed the headphones on Nick's head.

A sudden feeling of panic engulfed him. 'No. Those will make me feel more trapped.'

'OK, keep very still and hold your breath when we ask you.'

Nick tried to distract himself by thinking of his dinner date that night with Grace. He'd discovered that Danesh was going to be out and had suggested that Ben take Marcel out to a film and for a Nando's afterwards. The softener was a fifty-pound note he had placed in Ben's hand. Although it was a school night for Marcel, Grace had been surprisingly agreeable to the idea. But he soon succumbed to his claustrophobia. He made a mental note to remind Ben, if the worst came to the worst, to ensure he was really dead before he went in his coffin. Being burned alive is one thing, but buried alive is another.

In another hospital, on the other side of the River Thames, Kitty Lawrence was ready for discharge. The treatment from a rather handsome Kiwi physiotherapist had improved her mood, not to mention her mobility. When a smiley occupational therapist from Malaysia had suggested she undergo a home visit to see whether she could cope, Kitty had refused and demanded a stay in convalescence, only to be told in no uncertain terms by Sister McPherson (the Tyrone Terror as she was known among her staff) that no such thing had been available for over 30 years. Kitty, she announced, was becoming institutionalised. It was true that Kitty had grown surprisingly fond of her fellow patients. There was Irene, who had been admitted with a horrendous bedsore and, on being told that the hospital photographer wanted to take a picture of her, employed the institution's hairdresser for a cut and blow dry. After the photographer had departed Kitty discovered Irene in tears. 'It wasn't my face he wanted,' she cried. 'He took a close-up of my bum.' The woman in the bed next to her was occupied by the wife of a white hunter, whose husband attempted to pin a tiger skin above his spouse's bed, 'to make her feel at home'. Sister McPherson had had a fit when she discovered the old boy up on one of the hospital chairs juggling the skin and a hammer.

And now an earnest young doctor had come to see her to explain that she was now blocking a bed, which was costing taxpayers a lot of money.

'Young man, how old are you?'

'I'm twenty-four.'

'I presume you are happy to receive your training at taxpayers' expense.'

'Well, I've had to pay—'

'And how much tax have you actually paid? Don't tell me – very little. And I don't suppose you ever paid tax on your paper round or whatever you did before going to medical school. I, on the other hand, have been filling the taxman's coffers for over sixty years, so please don't start giving me lectures. And don't you dare refer to me as being a bed-blocker. That is quite insulting.'

'I'm sorry, Kitty.'

'Miss Lawrence to you. I won't be patronised because I am sixty years older than you.'

'I'm sorry, Mrs Lawrence. I never like to raise the issue of taxpayers but – my consultant told me to mention it.'

'Then she should have come and told me herself. Is she that bleached-blonde, po-faced woman? I didn't like her from the start.'

'Don't you want to go home?'

'Of course I do. I'd be delighted to leave this hospital, but only when I'm ready.'

'Is there anyone who can help you at home?'

'No. I live alone. Ernest and I were unable to have children. No productions of my own, I could say.'

'Is there anywhere you can stay for a few weeks until you have your confidence back?'

'My dear boy, don't talk to me about confidence. Have you ever played Desdemona at the National Theatre opposite Olivier?'

'I was in a few medical school revues—'

'Exactly.'

'What about' – the doctor steeled himself for the response – 'a residential home . . . just for a short period?'

'You're a very sweet boy. I know you're doing your job. I need a few more weeks until I'm back on my feet again. Literally. Now please leave me in peace. I'm sure you have other patients in much worse condition than me to attend to.'

Kitty turned away and faced the wall. Despite her bravura, she had never thought it would come to this. Oh, how she missed Ernest. Some tasks were becoming impossible, and living alone now seemed too much of a struggle. She turned back to gaze at his photograph on the bedside table.

She had met Ernest Forbes-Barrington at a labyrinthine antiquarian bookshop in Bloomsbury. Kitty didn't manage to find a rare early edition, but she did pick up the leading man in her life.

Ernest had been delighted when Kitty later agreed to marry him, but had never come to terms with the fact that she wouldn't take on his name. She could never be Kitty Forbes-Barrington. For one thing her adoring public had always known her as Kitty Lawrence, and for another, when it came to billing, it would have cost the theatre management a fortune in light bulbs. A single tear trickled down her cheek, leaving a line in her make-up. She couldn't let her public see her like this.

10

'Mmm – this is really good.' Grace savoured a mouthful of the chicken cacciatore. 'You can cook.'

'It's my signature dish. In fact, my only dish.' Nick refilled her glass from the particularly classy Burgundy she'd brought. Nick was by no means a fashionista, but he knew enough to know that she looked particularly lovely tonight in that elegant, midnight blue velvet cocktail dress. And those eyes . . .

'So, how are you getting on with Danesh?' Grace asked.

'Fine. He's a nice boy. Is he going to be able to stay in the UK?'

'It's in the balance. Anyway, it's good of you to have him stay here.'

'He's no trouble. He loves his telly, although he finds it funny that I still watch stuff on the old cathode ray.'

'His English is certainly improving.'

'That will be from *Countdown*. He's very impressive with unusual words.'

'Where is he tonight?'

'Don't know, but when he said he was going out I was pleased.'

'And it was lovely that Ben has taken Marcel to the cinema. It makes him feel grown-up. It's usually me that takes him out.'

'He's genuinely fond of Marcel. He doesn't spend time with him because he feels he should. They talk a lot.'

Grace was intrigued. 'Oh?'

'Well, Marcel was telling Ben that he wished he didn't have Down's syndrome.'

Grace sat back and folded her arms. 'You think we haven't had this conversation?'

'Yes, of course, I just thought—'

'There are things he can't do, but on the whole he's secure.'

'Oh, I know.' Nick wished he'd never mentioned Ben and Marcel's conversation.

'He's not defined by the Down's syndrome, although it obviously affects his day-to-day life. On the whole I think he's very happy, don't you?'

'I've never met anyone with such a zest for life.'

'Someone once said to me – a counsellor, funnily enough – that Marcel would never really enjoy his birthdays because he had Down's syndrome; he'd know that his birth had been greeted with anxiety and negativity. He was only two ... It broke my heart. And now he plans his birthdays for months ahead – you've never seen anyone so excited. Marcel surprises me every day. It's the attitude of other people that's the problem. Soon after his birth, a friend even said to me, "Do you cover his face when you take him out?"'

Nick raised his eyes heavenwards.

'Of course, it was difficult at first – especially when my partner had gone. But if Marcel didn't have Down's syndrome he wouldn't be the boy he is today. Another thing that really annoys me is when adults with learning difficulties are described as having the mental age of a child. Marcel is fourteen, but he has the emotional intelligence of someone much older. Sorry for the speechifying. Anyhow' – Grace reached across the table and rested her hand on Nick's wrist – 'As much as I love my son I didn't come here to talk about *him*.' She gave Nick a look that went straight to his knees.

'Didn't you?' He was relieved that he didn't have to talk about Marcel, but slightly perturbed at Grace's change of mood. He stared down at her hand as if she was checking his pulse.

'I like you, Nick. And I know you feel the same.'

'I do, Grace.' Nick was flummoxed. How did she know? He'd never dared broach the subject with anyone other than Deirdre.

'There's something I need to tell you, Grace. I've definitely got prostate cancer.'

'I had been wondering. I'm so sorry, Nick. How long have you known?'

'Not long. I wasn't sure when to tell you.'

'Well, I'm glad you have. There's no need to feel ashamed.' Grace had wondered quite how long Nick was going to keep the diagnosis from her, but she understood how difficult this was for him. She squeezed his hand harder. She was looking at him intently. Normally he would have needed little to react to a beautiful woman like Grace, but his life was in a mess. He hadn't wanted to involve her. He averted his gaze.

This was getting very awkward. Grace was wondering if

Junior had got the wrong end of the stick. She unfolded her napkin and brushed her mouth. 'Perhaps we should talk about *your* son now.'

'I'm sorry, Grace. It's just that . . .'

'It's OK.' Grace took a swig of wine. 'I thought . . . Never mind.'

The uncomfortable silence was suddenly broken by the doorbell being rung with some intensity. Talk about being saved by the bell.

'Good evening, Mr Greenwood.' The heavily accented voice of Bogdan boomed out of the intercom. 'We are here for you.'

Now it was Leon. 'Let us in, please.'

'No, no, no – this isn't—'

'Bogdan isn't used to being told no. You've said it three times.'

'No, I—'

'Four . . . He's also not very sensitive when it comes to doors being shut when he wants them open.'

'OK, OK!'

Bogdan and Leon strode into the hallway.

'Look,' gabbled Nick, 'I have a friend over for dinner.'

The two brushed past him. Bogdan looked approvingly at Grace and said, 'Very nice.'

Grace indicated the two heavies. 'Friends of yours?'

Leon looked expectantly at Nick.

'Yes. Friends. Normally I'm *delighted* to see them.'

'Mr Greenwood, you have date?' Bogdan asked doubtfully.

'No,' said Grace just as Nick was saying 'Yes', and then 'No!'

'Early days,' said Leon. Leon looked to Bogdan, who nodded, and the three of them went outside.

'Please, not tonight.' Nick looked pleadingly at Leon. 'Mr Robertson would understand.'

Leon turned to his sidekick. 'Do you think Mr Robertson would understand?'

'What does he want, Leon?'

'He's still waiting to hear from you about his daughter. And if you've had your money from Moran. Says he forgot to ask you.'

'Why does Charlie want to know?'

'Big believer in fairness,' said Bogdan.

'What does that mean?'

'We're just watching Moran. So far, that is,' Leon whispered. The two men laughed.

'What was that?' Nick was becoming a little concerned.

'Mr Greenwood, please answer question. Have you had money?'

'No, I haven't.'

'Dear, oh dear,' said Leon. The two henchmen looked at one another.

'Listen to me. Please don't do anything silly. I've already had a little run-in with the police. I don't want any more trouble.'

'We don't like trouble neither. Do we, Bogman?'

'I *concur*. You like my new word? I learned from Judge Rinder.'

Nick was becoming more anxious. 'Please, guys. Go home. Do it for me.'

A genuinely baffled Leon shrugged. 'We work for Mr Robertson – isn't that right, Bogman?'

'I concur. But we go find Steve Moran and maybe we come back. What about Ashley?'

'I'm still trying to find her.'

Leon shook his head doubtfully. 'I suggest you keep trying. When that nice lady tires of you, tell her I am available.'

Nick returned to the kitchen tapping furiously at his mobile. 'Grace, I must just make this call . . .'

At home in Tu Lions, Charlie Robertson was gently engaged in his daily backstroke lengths of his indoor pool, gazing up at the mock Sistine Chapel ceiling painted by his mate 'Fingers' Chapman. He'd done a good job, though some of the cherubs looked a little like some of their one-time confederates south of the river. And Noah bore a striking resemblance to Ronnie, or was it Reggie? When Fingers came out he'd have a word about a retouch.

All was very well with Charlie. His business activities were extremely profitable; his golf game was the best of his life — he was now playing off 16; his gorgeous new girlfriend Shazza was in the kitchen cooking his favourite chicken cacciotore — Charlie had got the recipe from Nick, who still hadn't come up with Ashley's daily whereabouts. Still, his daughter seemed as happy as ever. Decent bloke, Nick, but a bit of a plum at times. It would have been a nice little earner for him, but now he'd have to get Nick's sweetener back. It was looking as though Charlie was going to have rely on Bogdan and Leon after all — but they did tend to get a bit carried away with their work and he didn't want to cause his precious daughter any embarrassment. But he would help Nick with Steve Moran — jumped-up wankers like that got on his nerves. Then he'd have Leon and Bogdan turn their attention to Ashley. Only another 15 lengths to go. Yes, all was well in Charlie's world. Deep in thought and splashing loudly, he was oblivious to his mobile phone ringing deep in the pocket of his Tommy Hilfiger bathrobe hanging on the back of the sun bed.

Outside the Ministry of Soul nightclub in Soho Steve Moran, a little worse for wear, stumbled past a couple of bouncers hoping to pose for some fans seeking selfies. They never materialised. Their loss. He staggered up a dimly lit alley juggling with his mobile, which he then dropped. As he bent down a gloved hand reached for it. 'Please, Mr Moran, allow me.'

Steve Moran swung around to see Bogdan polishing the mobile. 'Thanks, pal. Butterfingers me, eh?'

Moran reached out for his phone, but Bogdan's only response was a menacing smirk. 'When I am ready.'

The actor took a step towards Bogdan. 'Now don't give me any trouble.'

'He won't give you any trouble.' From the other side of the alleyway Leon stepped into the light. 'Well, look, Bogman. The one off the telly.'

Moran shrugged. 'This is where I say, you want my autograph, and you say, no, your wallet. Right?'

'Very wrong,' said Bogdan. 'We have request.'

'Oh yeah?' Moran backed off a little as Leon and Bogdan circled him.

'You know Mr Greenwood? Nick Greenwood?' Leon removed his shades.

'That loser? Of course.'

Bogdan clasped his knuckles together. 'You owe Mr Greenwood money.'

Leon grasped Moran's sleeve. 'And he'd like you to pay up.'

'You mean he actually hired you goons? What are you, TV extras?'

Bogdan and Leon exchanged glances.

'Well, you tell Greenwood he gets nothing from me,' Moran went on. 'And if he makes trouble, I know some real hard men, not like you fucking snowflakes.' Moran turned to go but changed his mind. 'Pass this on to him.' He pulled his arm back and punched Bogdan as hard as he could in the stomach.

Bogdan didn't flinch. Moran was bent over in agony clutching his hand.

'*Jesus.* You got a gun under there?'

Leon was laughing loudly. 'Bogman, told you that six-pack of yours should be registered as a dangerous weapon.' Suddenly serious, he added, 'We don't carry guns around plonkers like you. You just broke your hand on solid Romanian marshmallow.'

'Well, if you're not armed, I'm walking away,' gasped Moran. 'Fuck off!' He took a step backwards, tripped over the kerb and was launched backwards into the road just as a van was speeding along. There was a screeching of brakes, an ear-piercing scream and a heavy thud. Leon and Bogdan stood impassive.

'Oops.' Bogdan stared at his friend. 'What do you think?'

'I know a good kebab shop in Tottenham.'

As the shocked van driver jumped out of his vehicle, head in his hands. Leon glanced at the blood-spattered body and then he and Bogdan strolled to their car. Leon looked back, and muttered, 'FIDO.'

'Leon, what do you talk about, *FIDO*?'

'Been learning some old gangster lingo from Charlie. Fuck It Drive On.'

Kitty was sitting beside her hospital bed reading the *Stage*. She glanced up to acknowledge her visitor with a royal wave. 'Extraordinary that they still allow Cissy Chipchase to tread the boards. She was past it when she appeared in that dreadful *Driving Miss Daisy* at the Criterion. They had to pay the prompt woman overtime.'

'Good afternoon, to you too, Kitty.' Sam handed Kitty a spectacular bouquet.

'Oh, Sam, what lovely flowers! That's much better. White gardenias. I made everyone wear one at Ernest's funeral.' She placed the spray carefully on her bed.

Sam pulled up a chair. 'How are you, Kitty?'

'At a bit of a stand-off, I'm afraid. They want to send me home. And I don't feel quite ready.'

'Not like you, Kitty.'

'They really are lovely flowers.'

'You could go somewhere just for a few weeks until you find your feet.'

'I knew where my feet were until that writer came to see me.'

Sam examined his nails before daring to ask the next question. 'What about convalescence – just for a few weeks?'

Kitty gave him a withering look. 'Aren't those places very expensive?'

'You have the money, Kitty.'

'I do not like the idea of being surrounded by people who don't understand the theatre. "Civilians", we used to call them.'

'I know just the place for you. Look, I've brought you a brochure.'

'Footlights House. I've heard of that. Isn't it full of old crocks?'

'Yes, but they've all been in the business – some still are. Look at the lovely grounds. The rooms have sea views.'

'It does look nice . . .' Kitty paused. 'Let me think about it.'

Nick had been trying to arrange another interview with Frankie Morrison, but there was always some excuse: trouble with my drains; head isn't in the right place; behind on my Pilates exercises. Most unbelievably, 'I've twisted my ankle on my run. Haven't been in such pain since I caught the clap from a Geisha girl in Yokohama.' The Geisha girl bit was probably true, and something to ask Frankie about later – he might get half a page out of it. But Frankie's latest excuse had alerted Nick to a fund of possible material. Aslan's Roar were having a first rehearsal for their forthcoming tour, and Nick seized the opportunity and invited himself along.

He was expecting some upmarket studio in Soho or the latest set up in Hoxton, but found himself in a draughty church hall in Pinner. Frankie told him Harvey Love, his arch nemesis, had got them a cheap rate. The two guitarists greeted each other with bear hugs and pats on the back that only men can confer on one another.

Two members of the band were catching up on old times with Frankie: ultra-tanned bass guitarist Bruce Jack had just flown in from his Malibu home. 'Guys, I'm just overwhelmed,' he gushed in a mixture of Govan and southern California. 'I love you both so much. This is super-awesome.'

Pasty-faced Dec Pertwee the rhythm guitarist, on the other hand, hailed from Welwyn Garden City and still resided there, and was altogether more Home Counties grounded. 'We haven't started yet, Bruce.' He aimed a thumb at Nick. 'Who's he?'

'This is Nick,' said Frankie. 'We're writing my autobiography.'

Dec snorted with laughter. 'Your autobiography? Who's going to want to read that, Frankie?'

Nick shrugged. 'I think Frankie still has quite a following. And he's had what we in the trade call "a life fully lived".'

'You're not exactly Keith Richards, though, are you, Frankie? This isn't Nellcôte.'

Frankie looked disdainfully at Dec. 'Well, if we were the Stones and rehearsing *Exile on Main Street* we might be able to rent a chateau on the Côte de fucking Azur.'

'Guys, the main thing is we're all together.' Bruce offered both hands for high fives.

'Apart from Harvey,' said Dec. 'Where is he anyway?'

'Didn't you have a falling out, Frankie?' said Bruce.

'Yeah, over Milly.'

'Stealing a band member's woman', Dec said. 'So uncool.'

'What are you talking about? There was a lot of swapping of birds in the band.'

'Sometimes the birds swapped us for other birds.'

'Harvey's probably buying gaffer tape. Bruce, do you remember when he bound you to a hotel bed with gaffer tape and smothered you with honey?'

'And let loose all those ants,' said Frankie.

'You left me there all day! Bitten all over, I was.'

'Remember when he rode his Harley through that hotel in Palm Springs and crashed into the lift?'

'Threw all my clothes into the swimming pool. And I was wearing some of them at the time. Happy days . . .'

Nick turned on his digital recorder. This was going to be a useful session.

As the three musicians plugged in their amps and tuned up with a few riffs there was the sound of the church hall door crashing open. In came a middle-aged, chubby woman in a voluminous daffodil-motif dress lugging a bass drum.

Frankie looked aghast. 'Christ, that isn't Milly? Glad I got out of that one.'

The woman was followed by a pony-tailed, leather-faced man in his seventies.

'Fuck me, what's he got round his neck?'

'A dog collar, Frankie,' Bruce said. 'Didn't you know Harvey's a man of God now? Trained for the ministry.'

'Always suspected this might happen,' Dec went on. 'Don't you remember? He was playing with some band at the Hammersmith Odeon when a spotlight came down and just missed him. He said it was a miracle. Turned his back on rock and roll – the Devil's music had ruined his life. Well, and the drugs. And the women.'

'So how come he's agreed to play again?' Nick piped up.

'Vicars don't earn much bread,' said Bruce. 'So that must be Karen. Harvey met her at a church social.'

Frankie proffered his hand and Harvey smiled beatifically. 'Bless you, Frankie.'

'Yeah, right. Your Holiness.'

'He's not the fucking Pope,' said Dec.

'Good afternoon.' The drum carrier addressed the group. 'I'm Karen.'

'I didn't know we were bringing spouses,' said Frankie.

Harvey put his arm around his wife. 'Karen's agreed to be our manager.'

Frankie was the first to react. 'What the fuck, Harvey?'

Nick checked his recorder and typed away furiously on his laptop. This was pure gold.

'Come on guys, we've only got the hall for three hours.' With Karen's help, Harvey set up his drum kit and the three guitarists each suggested a song to start with.

'"Wizards of the Golden Age"?'

'I could never bear that.'

'We've gotta do "Love is Painful".'

'Fuck off! Reminds me of when I had the clap. Sorry, Karen.' Frankie raised his hands in apology.

'For old times' sake I think we should ease ourselves back into the groove with "Into the Great Blues Yonder".'

'Oh, yeah? Well, that's not going to happen. It's always about you, isn't it, Dec?'

'I remember why we split up now,' said Bruce.

Karen suggested starting the session with a prayer, which was met with stunned silence. Then Nick's presence was objected to, and a couple of band members threatened to end the session if he didn't hand over his recorder and leave. 'We've lost millions in bootlegs,' said Dec, standing over Nick threateningly. 'None of this is for the book, right?'

'Of course,' Nick mumbled, meaning quite the opposite, but agreed to go. At last he'd got enough material to breathe some life back into Frankie's book. Later he'd learn from Frankie that the reunion had ended in a fist fight between Dec and Harvey and what Bruce described as 'some kind of stoochie', in which Dec had threatened Harvey with the same mysterious demise as two of the *Spinal Tap* drummers.

11

Several nights later, about 3 a.m., Nick woke up with a jolt, dripping wet. He had been warned that the medication would bring on hot sweats – making him much more sympathetic to women going through the menopause. As he lay there, recovering, he realised that this was not just a side effect of the female hormones he had been prescribed. It was a vivid nightmare, which slowly came back to him.

Confusing images of Amy. He was looking at a photograph of her on which her face had been covered in green ink. Then they were making love on a beach, and suddenly she had walked into the sea and disappeared. Somehow he knew she had drowned.

More elements of the dream slowly came back to him: images jumbled up with soldiers beating him with their batons.

No doubt Deirdre would want to hear about this, but first he wanted see Kitty.

When Nick arrived at the hospital later that morning Kitty was sitting in a chair by her bed, reading. 'I didn't expect you today. Come to apologise again?'

'No, that wasn't my reason for coming. But I will if you want me to.'

'What *was* your reason for coming?'

'I need to talk to you about your grandfather.'

'Why?'

'I've been dreaming about him, and I can't work out why. I thought you might be able to help me.'

'I thought I told you—'

'Please, Kitty, please.'

Kitty stared at Nick, lips pursed. 'Very well.' She left a dramatic pause. 'We were very close. He was in the First West Kents and served at Mons. Marvellous man. Survived the war, but barely spoke about it in later life.'

Nick nodded. 'That was the norm.'

'Yes.' Kitty was silent in thought. 'There was something else,' she eventually went on, looking out of the window. 'Something that he did talk about. I think about it every time I look at his photograph. Someone he killed.' She glanced at Nick. 'Perhaps I have said enough.'

'It was war. He must have killed many—'

'This was one of his own men. A friend. Both his legs had been blown off, and half his face was missing from a shrapnel wound. He wouldn't have survived. And he was in agony. Somehow he begged Grandpa to shoot him, and Grandpa did.' Kitty undid and then refastened a button on her cardigan. 'He used to have nightmares about it. But he knew he'd done the right thing. Perhaps that's why he had to talk about it.'

'And the authorities never found out?'

'Not to my knowledge.'

'A mercy killing.'

Kitty nodded slowly. 'Indeed. A humane act among much

inhumanity.' She paused. 'Sometimes you have to do terrible things for the right reasons.' She fixed Nick with a stare. 'This isn't for the book, Nick.'

'I understand, Kitty.' When a subject said, 'This isn't for the book,' then it usually was, but in this case he wouldn't insist. Even so, Kitty's words were ringing in his ears.

Ben was in when Nick got back home, but there was no sign of Danesh – again.

'He's seeing a lot of that author of yours,' Ben told his father.

'Which one?'

'Elysha.'

'It's more than I am. I still haven't met her. Still, that's interesting.'

'Is it? I think he might be taking advantage of her.'

'"Taking advantage"?' That's a curiously old-fashioned phrase, Ben! Have you been reading Jane Austen?'

'I mean I think he might be harassing her.'

'Really?'

'I think you need to have a word.'

'Don't be ridiculous.'

'She's your client. You're responsible for her welfare.'

'Ahh.' Nick finally realised what was going on. 'You know what I think, Ben?'

Ben was blushing. 'I'm just aware of how predatory men can be.'

'I think you like her.'

'You're being ridiculous, Dad.' Ben changed the subject. 'I'm going to be away for a couple of days – there's an occupation at college. And the other the thing is . . . I need a loan. Better still, a donation.'

'What is it this time? Should I be sitting down to hear this?'

'Fifty quid. More would be welcome.'

'What for?'

'A campaign at uni.'

'Go on.'

'Well, you won't believe this, but some people think it's OK to wear sombreros on campus. We want them banned.'

'The people?'

'The sombreros!'

'Even when it's hot?'

'No, *not* just when it's hot – the weather doesn't matter. Wearing sombreros if you're not Mexican reinforces stereotypes.'

'What happens if some of the students are Mexican?'

'There aren't any.'

'Well, that *is* discriminatory. Maybe you should be running a campaign to admit more Mexican students.'

'Dad, you're being ridiculous. This is cultural appropriation at its worst.'

'What?'

'Adopting a minority culture as your own.'

Nick was genuinely bemused. 'Isn't it a compliment? A nod in the direction of someone else's culture? Surely that's a good thing?'

'It's disrespectful and exploitative. You don't get it.'

'Wearing a sombrero? Well, I'll be dipped. Look, I've seen

Viva Zapata twenty-three times, and if being a Mexican was good enough for Marlon Brando – didn't I give you some money recently for another campaign?'

'That was for preventing Germaine Greer from speaking.'

'I gave you money for that?'

'The Students Union has passed a motion that "Germaine Greer is traitorous to her gender and toxically transphobic."'

'This is unbelievable, Ben. I'll have you know I've always considered myself something of a radical. In my formative years I always had a copy of *The Female Eunuch* in my jacket pocket.'

'Don't tell me you were a feminist?'

'That's where you're wrong. In the Seventies no man worth his salt would dare describe himself as a feminist. Calling ourselves "semi-liberated" was as far as we could go. The radical feminists – especially the shaven-headed lesbians – would have torn us limb from limb. Don't tell me you think Martina Navratilova is transphobic?'

'Definitely.'

'Martina Navratilova?' Nick was outraged. 'She's a gay icon! She's always fought for equality and gay rights.'

Ben shook his head. 'Says the man who described lesbians as "baritone babes"! She accused transgender women of cheating when they take part in women's sport. She's perpetuating transphobic myths.'

Nick was beginning to get annoyed.

'And it's an insult to my friends who are transitioning.'

'Which friends?'

'Well, one friend. Remember LaToyah?'

'Vaguely.'

'He's now known as Keith.'

Nick burst out laughing. 'I'm not against gender fluidity. It's calling herself Keith.'

'She's calling *himself* "Keith".'

'I thought you said it was one friend.'

'If you're confused, how do you think they felt when they were in the wrong body?'

'So *they* are becoming Keith? Sometimes I think I was born into the wrong brain.'

'Don't be crass, Dad. "*They*" is Keith's referred pronoun.'

'Look, Ben, I wish him, her, they well with his, her, their transitioning. Good luck to them. What are your preferred pronouns?'

'He, him, of course.'

'That's a relief.'

Now Ben was annoyed. 'Why is that a relief?'

'Having one child is quite expensive enough. I'm not giving you any money for banning sombreros.'

Ben shook his head despairingly and headed for his bedroom. The door slammed shut, and through it Nick could hear, 'For fuck's sake, Dad, you're just a Neanderthal.'

'I'm surprised you write off the underdog, Ben,' Nick called after him. 'It's been proven – we knuckle-draggers have quite big brains.' He slumped down on the sofa and switched on the television, which happened to be in the middle of the news.

NEWSREADER: . . . And over to Kosi Agbani, who is at the scene.

REPORTER: It was about ten p.m. last night when the van driver coming along this road saw three men having what appeared to be an altercation at the roadside. As he approached, one of the men seemed to fall into the path of a vehicle. He was killed instantly. The driver stopped, but the two other men, described by witnesses as being in their thirties, one of Afro-Caribbean appearance and the other white, left the scene. The victim turned out to be the actor Steve Moran, best known for playing Eddie Dunn in the soap *Southerners*. Coincidentally and tragically, his character recently suffered startlingly similar death recently. Back to you, Rick.

NEWSREADER: That's the actor, Steve Moran, who has died at the age of thirty-seven.

The following morning Nick opened his front door to two police officers. The burly male introduced himself as DC Martin; the other was WPC Mackenzie, who had arrested him at the bookshop: 'Mr Greenwood?'

'Well, obviously.'

'No need to take that tone.' DC Martin gave Nick a stern look.

'I am not taking a tone. That's just the way I talk,' Nick replied. 'I admit it has got me into trouble at times, but there you are.'

'We'd like you to come down to the station,' WPC Mackenzie said gently, 'and answer a few questions.'

'What for?'

'We'll tell you when we get there. '

'Do I need a solicitor?'

'No need to get briefed up at this stage,' said DC Martin, before adding, 'but you might later.'

At the station he was greeted by Sergeant Finchley with an affable, 'Oh hello, it's you again.'

Nick was confused, 'Am I being arrested?'

'No, not yet. We just want to interview you to eliminate you from our enquiries.' Nick was led into the same room where he had been taken after the Scrimshaws debacle. Two plainclothes detectives were awaiting his arrival.

The detective switched on a recording machine. 'I am DI Honeybourne and this interview with the suspect is being recorded in the presence of DS Fielding.'

'*Suspect*?' A shocked Nick stood up.

'Sit down, please, Mr Greenwood.'

The two officers spoke in turn.

'Mr Greenwood, you have no doubt heard about the death of Steve Moran.'

Nick rallied to convey an expression of extreme sympathy. 'Yes. Shocking. I was devastated.'

'We're investigating the circumstances of his death.'

'It was an accident, wasn't it?'

'We're not so sure.'

'We've interviewed the driver. Poor bloke. We have no information that he was driving in a dangerous manner. He told us he thought he saw someone had pushed Mr Moran in front of his van. Was that you, Mr Greenwood?'

'Of course not! You told me to stay away from him! And I have, believe me.'

'Can you tell me where you were last night?'

'At home.'

'Was anyone with you?'

'No, I was alone.'

'You seem to have been very angry with Mr Moran at Scrimshaws bookshop, and now, just a few days later, he's been killed in an accident.'

'Look, I was furious with him, but not enough to be involved in anything like this.'

'But you had a grudge against Mr Moran. It doesn't look very good, does it?'

'I've no idea how it looks to you, but this accident had nothing to do with me.'

'We've recovered Mr Moran's mobile phone. Perhaps you'd like to listen to this.

Hi, Steve. It's Nick, your non-existent ghost writer here. How are you? Well, I know how you are because I'm watching you live on TV right now, lying through your shiny white veneers. Which I don't really care about as much as I care about you not paying me the money *you owe me for making your* miserably dull life *marginally* more interesting *than I find watching you* act. *Except for watching your death on TV last night, which I must say I* really enjoyed, *and which I'm hoping was just a rehearsal for the* real thing.

'Would you like to comment?'

Nick was flustered. 'Well, of course, I didn't *mean* it! I was angry with him.'

'Bit of a coincidence, don't you think?'

'Yes, that's all it is. Coincidences do happen. I had nothing to do with this. I'm not that stupid. Don't you have CCTV of what happened?'

'We're working on it. But we have looked at other footage, and are aware of a vehicle seen leaving the area at great speed soon after, which belongs to a Mr Leon King. Do you know who he is?'

Nick's heart sank. 'Um . . . sort of.'

'What do you mean, "sort of"?'

'He's not my mate, but I—'

'There were two men in the car. Leon King is an associate of Charlie Robertson, who is well known to us. And known to you. Could he be the other man?'

'No. Absolutely not.' At least Nick could reply with a clear conscience.

'We'll investigate further, of course.'

'Of *course*.' Nick pretended he was delighted, but he was already terrified about what they might find.

'The thing is, Mr Greenwood,' said one of the detectives as Nick got up to leave, 'you've got form, haven't you?'

'What are you talking about?'

'I'm referring to your late wife. You were divorced, weren't you?'

'Yes. But what on earth do you mean?'

'Two people known to you die within six months of each other.'

'She was ill!'

'If you say so.'

'I do say so.'

'We will be checking up on the circumstances of her death.'

'There's nothing to find. She died from a stroke.'

'We'll be checking the results of the post-mortem – closely. That's all for now, Mr Greenwood.'

Footlights House occupied the corner of a Georgian house on the seafront at Hove. Once owned by a theatrical impresario, the building had been purchased by a charitable organisation and converted into a residential home with 35 ensuite rooms for those who had made a living on stage or backstage – a mixture of retired theatricals and entertainers. Kitty had agreed somewhat reluctantly to a short stay until she felt able to cope in her flat. She was a little dismayed to find that variety entertainers were among the residents, but she felt confident of keeping them in their place.

The taxi driver extracted Kitty's walking frame and a large trunk from the boot. 'Why couldn't you get something on wheels, Kitty?' exclaimed Sam as he struggled to tow it behind him.

'Try breathing properly.'

Huddled together on a garden bench donated by the Vaudeville Benevolent Fund were Vernon Barrett, a bit-part actor in rep for many years and latterly in police and medical dramas, and his wife Charlotte, best known for her portrayal of Mrs Crabtree in the long-running radio series *The Foresters*. The inscription on the bench read, *In loving memory of Johnny Scott. A much-loved farceur and a joy to know.* Johnny Scott had been an impossible egocentric at whose memorial service at the Actors' Church there had been unrestrained joy.

Vernon doffed his trilby in Kitty's direction. 'Kitty! Kitty Lawrence! I don't believe it!'

Sam sank down on the trunk for a rest while Kitty looked the woman up and down. 'Do I know you?'

'Oh, we've never met,' said Charlotte. 'But I know your work. Are you coming to stay here?'

'For a short while.'

'We are honoured to have someone of your reputation here, aren't we, Vernon?'

Vernon raised his hat again and murmured sweetly, but vacantly, 'Yes, lovely. Quite lovely.'

The sitting room of Footlights House had the ambience of a not-so-grand hotel. It was comfortably furnished in contrasting styles; olde-worlde chintz met modern Scandi and soft leather sofas mingled with sturdy orthopaedic chairs. The walls were festooned with numerous theatrical playbills bearing legendary names of the past, variety posters and sepia photographs of prominent performers. On another wall hung a series of original oil portraits of the celebrities who had donated money to the home and in return had rooms named after them, among them the actors Will Hay and Robert Donat, the impresario C. B. Cochran and, more recently, a surprisingly sizeable contribution from the entertainer Tommy Steele. A recreation room had been paid for by Sir Billy Butlin and the laundry room, ironically, by Max Miller.

Kitty and Sam were welcomed by the matron, a qualified

nurse in her early forties whose patience was often tried by the dramas enacted by the residents, and who found solace in the bottle of Kentucky sourmash kept in her medicine cabinet. 'We have about forty residents all needing differing levels of care,' she told them, 'and we like to think they're all treated equally.'

Kitty raised a critical eyebrow. 'You mean there aren't any "names above the title"?'

'Well, of course, we've never had anyone of your standing before, and when I dropped your name – *mentioned* your name – to the residents there was a chorus of approval.'

Sam didn't believe a word of this, but was grateful for the matron's theatrical knowhow. 'There you are, Kitty. I knew you'd be in good hands.'

'Miss Lawrence, let me introduce you to some of the residents. You must have met Edward Harcourt. I've asked him to join you.'

'*Teddy Harcourt* is here?'

'He's been here a few years. Charming man.'

'I wouldn't really know.' Despite her outward disinterest, Sam noticed a slight softening in Kitty's manner.

Sam took Kitty's arm as they made their way down the hallway. The two of them sat themselves down in comfortable armchairs while the matron dispatched one of the care staff, a failed female impersonator, to bring them tea and biscuits.

Almost immediately Kitty was approached by an elderly man, resplendent in yachting blazer, silk cravat and Panama jauntily perched on dyed blond hair.

'Hello, I would introduce myself, but I already know who I am.' The man, whose accent was unadulterated Wigan, paused for the laugh. None came, although Sam smiled politely. 'But just in case you don't know me,' the man continued, 'I'm Harry Hallyday. Every day's a Hallyday. A laugh, a song, a concertina.'

'Thank goodness he's lost his concertina,' said Kitty in a stage whisper.

'I'd like to welcome you here to our little abode. I expect you know of me. My summer show in Eastbourne, *Sparkles*, ran for twenty years.' Kitty's shake of the head didn't deter him. 'You know I was dame in Scarborough before my career came to an abrupt end.'

Winifred folded her arms and said, 'Oh, Harry, we've heard this story so many times before.'

Harry was unabashed. 'I was in Sherwood Forest. Not *the* Sherwood Forest, you understand. Panto. The dame. Oh, I'd played there for years. They loved me. *Babes in the Wood*. Suddenly the scenery collapsed. I always knew that one day I'd bring the house down.' Kitty gave Hallyday a look that had destroyed the careers of a number of principal boys. 'I was a year in hospital and then came here.' Kitty smiled disingenuously and offered no words of sympathy.

The matron, seeing Kitty wasn't in the mood for Harry Hallyday's predicament and less so for his patter, broke in. 'Harry, can you do me a favour?'

'Of course, my darling. For you anything. Look at her. Pretty as a picture and not a bad frame.' Harry kissed Winifred's hand.

'Trixie needs collecting.'

'Bloody hellfire! She hasn't gone missing again, has she?'

'Be a darling. I'll arrange a taxi – she's at the stage door of the Palladium again.'

Harry turned to Kitty. 'That's our Trixie. Trixie Tanner. The "Twinkle-Toed Tapper", still hoping to tap her way to stardom. She never was much good, but she's one of ours.'

'Often when she goes missing she's at the theatre,' said the matron, 'expecting to be appearing at the Saturday matinee.'

Harry was hardly out of earshot when Kitty turned to Sam. 'Dreadful man.'

'At least it won't be dull here, Kitty.'

'*If* I decide to come here.' Kitty was distracted by the arrival of a handsome silver-haired man attired in a smart lounge suit with more than a hint of Stewart Granger about him.

'Oh, Teddy, it's you!' She struggled to get to her feet.

'Please don't get up.' Edward Harcourt bent down to kiss Kitty. 'I think I can still bend down enough to greet you properly.'

'What a lovely surprise.'

'Kitty darling. I heard you were visiting. I couldn't wait to see you.'

'Sam, this is Edward Harcourt. We were in rep together.'

'A long time ago. I've been "resting" for years now.'

'What, here, at Footlights House?'

'I only came for a couple of weeks – and that was several years ago. You'll love it here, Kitty.'

'It's just an audition, Edward. I still have my home in Teddington.'

'Oh, Kitty. Can't believe my luck.' Edward Harcourt gripped Kitty's arm tightly. She placed her hand on his.

Sam raised his eyebrows in an inquisitive look, which was duly blanked by Kitty. 'Thank you for bringing me, Sam. I'm fine now. You can come back in a couple of hours and collect me.'

'But—'

'Why not go for a walk on the seafront? Teddy and I have a lot of catching up to do.'

12

The death of Steve Moran and the subsequent questioning by the police had left Nick in turmoil. He wasn't sure of his next move, but thought he had better check in with Clarissa, who had insisted they meet for breakfast at the Wolseley. Nick was happy to; it was one of his favourite places for a meal.

He ordered eggs Florentine and a macchiato and waited for Clarissa, who was fashionably late – she had texted him her order of smoked haddock kedgeree and a glass of prosecco. In the meantime he studied his phone for any details about Steve Moran's demise. One report caught his eye, which stated that 'a man aged 69 and known to Steve Moran has been helping police with the enquiries and released while further investigations take place.' Thank goodness the press hadn't got hold of his name, although there was no need to add five years to his age.

The sound of raised voices made Nick look up to see Clarissa with two large suitcases arguing with the maître d'. After a heated discussion, she came over and he rose to greet her with an awkward 'air' kiss. 'Stupid man. He didn't want to let Digby in. I told him he was my Hypo Hound.'

Nick looked down at a lethargic Yorkshire terrier.

'Are you diabetic?'

'Of course not. He's more of a support dog – you know, for when I get anxious – but Hypo Hound sounds more dramatic, don't you think?'

'I wouldn't have thought of you as an anxious type, Clarissa.'

Clarissa sat down just as their breakfast was delivered, looking battle-weary and angry. 'On occasions. And this is such an occasion.' She placed Digby delicately on her lap and, much to Nick's disdain, began to feed the Yorkie with minute titbits of her smoked haddock. 'This wasn't the ideal time for us to meet. I have had the week from hell. Do you know I received an email today from one of my authors who is being sued because he described a hell-raising actor as teetotal? And I seem to be spending an inordinate amount of time keeping Junior's publisher's happy in regard to the various people supposedly libelled in his book. That's not my job. That's your fault.'

Nick shrugged. Before he could offer any kind of defence Clarissa was off again. 'How on earth did you put up with him?'

'What?'

'I've got to get rid of him.'

'Who?'

'Your Junior.'

'He isn't *my* Junior. I kind of thought he was *your* Junior.'

'He's going too fast for me. He's besotted. He wants children. I mean, the sex is super-fantastic.' A look of fulfilment came across her. 'You'd never guess what he can do with—'

Nick held up his hands. 'Yes, all right, Clarissa.'

'How did I end up in this job? It's a nightmare. It's like God has taken the worst bits from the worst jobs imaginable and come up with the notion of "the literary agent". My life was never meant to be like this. And I swear if I have to go to another literary party, or book launch, or be wined and dined by some dull politician who's decided he'd rather be a novelist, I shall commit bloody murder.'

'Unfortunate choice of words.'

'Now I have to catch a train to Dorset, to spend the weekend in a boutique hotel courtesy of some knobhead of a chef who wants to write what amounts to a glorified recipe book. Anyway, what is it you wanted to talk to me about?'

'Well—'

'Come on, Nick, spit it out. I'm feeling very stressed. You're the one who wanted to meet. Oh, before I forget, I've been trying to contact Steve Moran. I left several messages, heard nothing back.'

'Probably because he's dead.'

'*What?*'

'Steve Moran is dead.'

Clarissa looked at him uncertainly. 'You mean, dead-dead?'

'Don't you ever look at the news?'

'Of course not. When was this?'

'Last night.'

'Oh my God.'

'Murdered, they reckon. The thing is, the police suspect me.'

Clarissa reacted with a mixture of excitement and horror. 'How extraordinary!'

'What?'

But she was on a roll. 'My dear Nicholas. One minute he's on the TV, the next he's dead. It's perfect publicity for the book.'

'Did you hear me say, "The police think I killed him"?'

'You'll be famous.'

'And probably in prison.'

'That is a slight inconvenience.'

'Fifteen years to life of inconvenience, at a guess.'

'Lots of time to write your next book. Ha!' She paused triumphantly. 'You do get yourself in some scrapes.' She reached across and took a forkful of food from Nick's plate. 'Digby loves spinach.'

Grace had become used to working from home during the pandemic, usually interviewing her clients on Zoom, but as Danesh was now living in the flat below she could talk to him face to face, which she much preferred. Danesh had read a story with Marcel, 'to improve my English', and Grace's son was now asleep.

'He is a lovely boy.'

'Thank you, Danesh.'

'Some people in my country would not accept him.'

'Well, he hasn't always been accepted here.'

Danesh shook his head. 'It is so cruel.'

Grace nodded. 'I've had some difficult times. But things are fine now – although I do sometimes worry about his future.'

'And you worry about my future too.'

Grace smiled. 'Yes, I suppose there are parallels.'

'Do you mind if I ask you about his father?'

'He left me when Marcel was born. It was lucky, really – it

would have been difficult for me to bring up two children on my own.'

'You have no boyfriend?'

'Danesh, I think this is getting a little too personal.'

'You like Nick?'

'Danesh!'

'I think you like him. He likes you.'

'You're not the first person to tell me. What is going on? I'm not sure Nick likes me in that way. It's so difficult to tell with him.'

'This sounds like the talk between two teenagers. He is a nice man. And very handsome.'

'Danesh, your asylum application—'

'Sorry, but I see a flame between you.'

'I think you mean spark. But . . . no, don't be ridiculous. We're just neighbours.'

'And friends.'

'Good friends.'

'Ben is my friend. He is also a good boy.'

'You think everyone is good or nice.'

'Not my traffickers. But I feel sorry for Ben.'

Grace did a double take. 'You feel sorry for *him*?'

Danesh shrugged. 'I know I am in difficult circumstances, but I have my mother. She is in Iran, but she is alive. Ben has no mother. Maybe he will have you for a mother.'

'I don't think so, Danesh.'

'It would be good. But he really needs a girlfriend.'

Grace smiled. 'You're becoming a one-man dating agency.'

'A girl with a bit of whizz-bang.'

'I've never heard it put like that!'

'There is a woman I like. And I think she likes me.'

'Oh? Do you want to tell me more?'

'No. We see.'

Grace opened up her iPad. 'Now I need to let you know what is happening with your asylum claim. This girl of yours – does she have whizz-bang?'

That night, to distract himself, Nick finally got around to reading the six chapters Elysha had emailed him. It was now after midnight and, despite everything, he was completely engrossed. He called Sam, who he knew would be up studying the *Racing Post*.

'I wish you wouldn't use Facetime at this time of night, Nick. I look like a cross between W. H. Auden and Edith Sitwell.'

There was no point in Nick denying this. 'I've just read the chapters this glamour model gave me.'

'And?'

'Well, I thought it would be a rubbish kiss-and-tell memoir, but it's a novel. I thought it would need a lot of work. But it's terrific! With a little guidance she could come up with something special. Would you have a look at it?'

'If it doesn't need much work, why don't you take it on?'

Nick scratched his head. 'I've got quite a lot on at the moment.'

'Pray tell.'

'The police are trying to link me to Steve Moran's death. It was in all the newspapers. If this book with the glamour model is a success, perhaps we could work out a deal. Anyway, can I send it you?'

'I suppose there's nothing to lose.'

Unable to sleep, Nick had woken early the following morning. He made himself a cup of coffee and sat in reflective mood. What could the police have meant about Amy's death by 'You've got form, haven't you?' And as for reopening the circumstances of her death . . . His gaze settled on a couple of old photo albums on the bookshelf. He pulled out one and flicked through the images of the two of them together in happier times. He was caught unawares by Ben entering the living room and attempted to snap the album shut. 'Oh – I thought you were at the occupation.'

'The university got an injunction. What were you doing, Dad?'

'Just looking through some old photos. Never mind now. Listen, we need to talk.'

'Oh, sorry, I emptied the fridge – thought I might need some sustenance.'

'Steve Moran is dead.'

Ben was genuinely surprised. 'Bloody hell. Your wish came true.'

'I didn't really want him *dead*.'

'Could have fooled me.'

'The thing is, Ben, while you were otherwise occupied yesterday morning, the police took me into custody. They think I had something to do with it.'

'Honest, Dad, I didn't tell them anything!'

Nick smiled before recounting the previous day's events. Ben's eyes grew wider with each detail. 'So they really do suspect you?'

'Yes. I promise you, Ben, I wasn't anywhere near Moran that night.'

'Sure, Dad. So what's going to happen?'

'I might have to go back for further questioning.'

'Have you told Grace? She's a lawyer.'

'It's not her type of law. And I haven't been charged yet. But I will tell her. Don't worry, it will be all right.'

Ben glanced at the photo albums. 'Let's have a look.'

Nick opened the album at random to reveal a snap of him, in purple loons, Afghan coat and a huge Iron Cross.

'I didn't know you were a Nazi.'

'I wasn't. That is embarrassing.'

'Not as embarrassing as your hair. What were you thinking of?'

'I know. I look like Rasputin.'

'Where was that taken? Woodstock?'

'School speech day. I did it for a bet. Your grandparents weren't impressed.'

Nick flicked through the album to reveal a young woman in a bikini giving the photographer a thumbs-up.

'Is that Mum? I haven't seen that one before.'

'We were in the Fig Tree café on the Venice Beach boardwalk. Just after we met.'

'Why did you come back from LA?'

'I got bored with casual work. And your grandmother was in poor health.'

There was a pause while Ben studied the image. 'I went to see Mum in hospital.' He looked to his father for a response.

Nick returned Ben's stare with a look of bewilderment. 'I didn't know about that.'

'Only once. It was during one of the Covid outbreaks. Don't know how I did it, but I snuck into her room.'

'Did she recognise you?'

'Don't think so. I wish I hadn't. It was really awful to see her like that.' Ben pursed his lips. 'Dad, I know she left us and everything, but I miss her. Does that sound funny?'

'Of course not. I'm glad you saw her before she died, even when she was so ill.'

'What did Mum die of?'

Nick snapped the album shut. 'I don't know. I think she had another stroke.'

'Poor Mum.'

'Yes, poor Mum.'

There was a momentary avoidance of each other's gaze.

'I know I've joked about your illness,' said Ben, 'but I don't want to be an orphan at twenty-one.'

'I promise you, Ben, everything will be all right. I'm not going to die soon or spend the rest of my days in prison.' He hugged Ben in a tight clinch. 'Please don't worry.'

He would do the worrying for both of them.

*

'How was the match, Marcel?'

'It was am . . . ma . . . mazing! Spurs scored three goals.'

'Unfortunately, so did West Ham.' Junior laughed and swapped fist pumps with Marcel. 'But I did manage to get him into the Tottenham dressing room after the match.'

'And I took some selfies. Look Mm . . . Mum!' Marcel adeptly flipped through a few images.

'And who's that?' Grace asked. 'He doesn't look very happy.'

'He wasn't.' Junior smiled.

Marcel frowned. 'He's a West Ham player. He came . . . c-came in to see a friend of his who played for Spurs.'

'And shall we tell your mum why he isn't looking happy?'

'If you like, J-Junior.' Marcel grinned with an air of devilment.

'Well, that was when—'

'I called him a wanker!'

'*What?* Where did you learn that?'

'From Junior.'

'Oy! No, you didn't, Marcel. Don't land me in it.'

Grace gave Junior a playful slap.

'It may have been his first match, but he soon caught on. And that wasn't the worst of it, was it, Marcel?'

'Going to play FIFA.' Marcel gave Junior a hug and swiftly departed.

'I'm sorry, Junior.'

'That's OK, Grace. We had fun, although I'm going to get some pelters from some of the West Ham lads when I see them. They thought it was a laugh. And then when he came across a group of Hammers fans on our way home, he—'

'I do not want to know. But thanks, Junior – he'll never forget this.'

'Neither will I.'

'Do you want to stay for a glass of wine?'

While Grace fetched a bottle from the fridge Junior took a seat at the kitchen table. 'Can I ask your advice, Grace?' Before Grace had time to respond he went on, 'I've been going out with this woman called Clarissa – she's Nick's agent – but last time I saw her it didn't go so well. She said she wasn't ready to settle down, she found me "immature" and – the worst thing – she criticised my charity work. My football foundation in Grenada.'

'Why would she do that?' Grace poured herself a glass of wine and joined Junior.

'She said charity begins at home, and that I was giving away too much of my money. I'm not even lying. Shame, I thought I was in love. Hundred per cent.'

'Lucky escape, from what I've heard about Clarissa.'

'I wanted kids with her.'

'Well, I wouldn't force the issue.' As soon as she said it Grace put her head in her hands and giggled.

Junior looked askance at Grace. 'Never mind. It's over.'

'Are you sure?'

'She told me she'd rather spend her life as a shrivelled-up old spinster.'

Grace nodded. 'It's over.' Junior's mournful expression prompted her to give him a hug, but their embrace was interrupted by Marcel, who had decided to raid the freezer for a Mini

Magnum. He took one look at them, and said, 'Junior, are you going to marry my mum?'

'Can I lie down?'

'Of course. I've been trying to get you to use the couch since our first session.'

'I was worried I might fall asleep. If I do doze off—'

'I'll make sure you won't.' Deirdre gave Nick a scary stare. 'Am I to guess there's a reason for this? Booking a double session?'

Nick stared at the ceiling and noticed a few cobwebs above the Munch print. 'I have a confession to make.'

'It won't be the first time. I am a therapist.'

'In fact, perhaps *you* should lie down on the couch.'

Deirdre tapped her pen on the table.

'I don't quite know how to put this, but . . .'

'Go on.'

'I murdered Amy.'

'*What?*' The pen had stopped tapping.

'What did you say?'

'I murdered Amy.'

'What are you talking about?' Deirdre looked at Nick in disbelief.

'It's true.'

'I'm really not sure you should be telling me this.'

'Neither am I.'

'*When?* When was this?'

'Six months ago.'

'So why are you telling me now?'

'I nearly confessed to you before, but it never seemed the right time. And now the police are investigating. I have to tell someone.'

Deirdre looked aghast. 'Maybe the police, Nick?'

'Don't be daft, Deirdre. Who else can I tell apart from you? I was feeling a bit guilty. But something someone told me has helped me.'

'A *bit* guilty! Are you serious, Nick?'

''Fraid so.'

Nick had now noticed some dust on the curtain rails. 'Do you know you should get a cleaner? The state of your consulting room is a bit disconcerting.'

'Nick, this is unbelievable.'

'It's all right, Deirdre. I won't tell your other patients you can't afford a cleaner.'

'That is not the response of a guilty man. Is this a joke?'

'I'm sorry. It happened. But I had no choice.'

Deirdre shook her head in disbelief, 'You know I have a duty to report this.'

'What about patient therapist confidentiality?'

'I'm not sure it extends to murders.'

'Only one murder of a previous partner. Not murders. I don't have several ex-wives in various hospitals awaiting my divine intervention.'

'One is enough.'

'Don't you have a handbook for this sort of thing?'

Deirdre regarded her patient disdainfully. 'No, Nick, we don't.'

'There must be some sort of organisation you belong to?'

'What would you like me to do? Put it out for general discussion?'

'You must talk to someone about your patients?'

'I have my own therapist.'

'There you are.' Nick had a thought. 'Hang on – you have to go through this yourself?'

'Of course. Every therapist worth their salt has their own therapist.'

'Oh. Kind of self-perpetuating, isn't it? What about her?'

'Him.'

'You want to watch out for transference, Deirdre. I hear it can be a problem.'

'Nick, we're getting off the subject. This is *incredibly* serious.'

'I pretended to be a doctor and sneaked into her hospital room.'

'You killed her because she ran out on you and Ben?'

'*No*. Not at all. This wasn't personal. I just couldn't let her live any longer.'

'I don't understand.'

'It wasn't an act of revenge, Deirdre. It was more that we had an understanding. It was an act of mercy. We agreed that if either of us ended in a vegetative state . . . well . . . we would do what we could to ensure, by whatever means, that the other's life would not be prolonged unnecessarily. In fact, we nearly wrote it into our marriage vows. Not very romantic, I grant you.'

'Whether legal or not.'

'Preferably legal, but whatever it took. Her mother in the

States wouldn't give permission to have the life support turned off, and I was no longer next of kin. The doctors had a duty to sustain Amy and she just wouldn't get a chest infection, which would have finished her off. I waited for several months after her stroke, and realised I had to do something.'

'Nick, this is extraordinary. Wasn't there a post-mortem?'

'No. There was no evidence of malpractice or foul play. I never understood about them not finding evidence of the latter.'

'I don't know what to say.'

'Tricky, isn't it?'

'And you thought you had got away with it?'

'Until now. I did a terrible thing for the right reason.'

'Nick, euthanasia is against the law whatever your motives might have been. You've put me in a very difficult position.'

'Oh, and you ought to know I'm also in the frame for another murder.'

'What are you talking about?'

'Steve Moran. Remember him?'

'Are you making all this up?' Deirdre was in a state of shock.

'No. But it's OK. The police know all about that one.'

13

Nick's confession had left him alternating between dread and euphoria. On leaving the session, he had asked the ashen-faced Deirdre not to go to the police about Amy. They were already involved. Deirdre had replied that she wasn't sure what she was going to do, and her usual 'Your time is up' seemed much more menacing than usual.

On his walk home he turned on his mobile phone and there was a voice message from Frankie that didn't altogether surprise him: 'Hi Nick, I need to talk. The tour is off. Professional and musical differences. Give me a bell.'

Nick rang him back straight away. 'What "professional differences"?'

There was a chuckle. 'Well, actually I decked Dec.'

Nick sighed. 'So now what?'

'It's no good. I can't go on with this book. I've had enough. I'm afraid I can't give you anything more.'

'Anything *more*?'

'I'm an empty vessel. I've run dry. I'm fucking done with it all. Bye.'

'Are you going to pay me for the work we've done?'

'Gotta go, Nick. See you around.'

'Wow, this is beautiful – what a gaff!' Sam had invited Elysha for lunch at his elegant Chelsea home to discuss her book, *Model Behaviour*. 'This is a bit like my dad's place, but I got to say, even more classy.' Elysha sat back and sipped from her Waterford cut-glass flute, which was gently fizzing with champagne. Surrounded by antique artefacts, velvet curtains, chandeliers the size of football pitches and Romanesque statues, she hadn't seen anything like it since being taken to the Victoria and Albert Museum on a school trip. 'I hope you don't mind me saying but this is ... well ... a bit over the top.'

Sam laughed. 'I know it's all a bit camp. I did inherit most of this from a gay actor friend of mine.'

'I'm a bit of a hoarder myself,' Elysha said.

Sam nodded understandingly. 'Shoes and handbags?'

'Is that what you think of me? Don't be a plum, Sam. Books. I love books. I can't move in my bedroom for books. Old-school, eh?'

'Talking of which—'

'Before we talk about my book, I want to make sure Nick is OK with you representing me.'

'I'll see him right. We're old friends.'

Elysha raised her glass to Sam. 'You also said you had some good news. I suppose that's the reason for the fizz.'

'It's actually wonderful news, my dear. I loved your

manuscript, and so did the publishers I submitted it to. In fact, we're now in the middle of a bidding war.'

Elysha sat forward in excitement. 'Oh, my days!'

'So' – Sam paused for dramatic effect – 'we're up to fifty thousand pounds, and I think we can squeeze a bit more out of them.'

'Fifty grand! Blimey! That's more than I earn in a year! How come they want my book so much?'

'Publishers are always on the look-out for new novelists – especially with your background.'

'They don't expect someone like me to have any brains.'

'Don't quote me, but I'm afraid that's true. We're possibly talking a three-book deal. Do you think you can manage that – when you've finished this one?'

'Course. I've got lots of ideas. And I could give up work. But you're sure Nick won't be cross?'

'Nick's absolutely fine about it, and besides, he's in a bit of shit at present.'

'Honestly – look at my trainer! Bloody animals!' Nick lifted one of his Nike Dunk Low Retros for Grace's inspection.

'Yes, I see it, thanks, Nick. Imagine animals defecating in the zoo.'

'I've a good mind to complain to the keeper.'

'Why have we come to the Touch Paddock? It's meant to be for kids.'

'I like goats. Monkeys make me nervous.'

'Well, you seem to have been on edge all morning. And nothing to do with the animals.'

Nick had decided to invite Grace to join him for a day at the zoo, thinking it would be a relaxing place to come to, but when Grace insisted on holding hands in the warmth of Butterfly Paradise, surrounded by dazzling, fluttering, tropical butterflies, Nick had become agitated and, for reasons best known to him, had decided to tell Grace about some of his previous girlfriends.

'And after Isabel, who dumped me for my best friend, I went out with Sarah, who happened to be General William Tecumsah Sherman's great-great granddaughter. Well, I didn't fare any better than Atlanta with her. Then I met a Chilean in a pub who thought my main interest in her was only that I was spying for General Pinochet. And that was the end of that.'

'Nick, please. Stop. I'm not sure I really want to hear about all your conquests. Would you like me to recite a list of my ex-partners? Not exactly the ideal way to romance me.'

'I'm sorry, Grace.'

'What's the matter with you? Every time I show a bit of affection, you withdraw and start rambling.' Grace shrugged. 'I'm pretty good at reading people, but you ...' Her voice trailed off.

'I'm a bit confused.' Nick faltered. 'The thing is, I'm not quite ready for sex.'

'I think you're thinking a little too far ahead, Nick. I'm not suggesting I take you into the Reptile House and have my wicked way with you.'

'Oh. That's a relief.'

'Well, that's good to know.' Grace folded her arms.

'Oh, I didn't mean that! I mean I would love to – of course – but . . .' He gazed at Grace fondly. 'It's just that . . . You see . . . now that my cancer has been confirmed, they have told me that my medication – oh, this very embarrassing – and so there'll probably be a loss of libido.'

Grace leaned towards Nick and pulled him by his coat lapels closer to her. 'Nick, I'm sorry to hear that, but I'd rather you were honest with me than telling me what an exciting time you've had with different women over the years.'

'I know. I know. It's ridiculous, but there is so much on my mind at the moment.'

'Please talk to me.'

Nick stared at her. She was right, of course. He didn't want to risk their relationship by admitting the deep trouble he was in, but knew he would have to tell her sooner or later.

He took Grace's arm and, as they strolled round the zoo, told her everything he had told Deirdre about the circumstances of Moran's and Amy's deaths and the subsequent police involvement. Every so often the two of them came to a halt to face one another and he let Grace ask him her questions.

The more he confided in Grace, the greater the relief he felt. Her grip on his arm became more vice-like as she listened to his confession with mounting incredulity.

When he'd finished, he looked deep into her eyes. There was a momentary silence, following which Grace raised her hands heavenwards. 'I don't know what to say.'

'That's exactly what my therapist said. And I'm paying good money for that sort of insight.'

'I don't think you should be telling me all this, Nick. I am a lawyer, after all.'

'I want to tell you everything from now on.' Nick released her grip and then wrapped his arms around her, kissing her gently on the mouth. Grace pulled back, her eyes narrowing. She stared at Nick in what seemed an interminable silence.

Now he had told her almost everything. But was this really the time to tell her how he felt about her? To declare his love in the environs of the Pygmy Hippos' Hot Tub seemed a little inappropriate.

Under investigation for involvement in two murders and in a whirl about his relationship with Grace, Nick decided he had to get away. With misgivings, he rang his father. 'Dad, I'd like to come and stay for a few days. Recharge the batteries.'

'That would be marvellous. And we could go and see Cecil about his book. He's getting a bit impatient with the lack of progress.'

Nick had forgotten all about this. 'Yes, we can do that, Dad.'

'You know, it's lovely down here at the moment. Or should it be up here? I've never really known. The daffodils are starting to bloom, the crocuses are out and the magnolia is glorious.' Richard began to hum the first few lines of 'English Country Garden'.

'OK, Dad, OK. Look, I'm getting the train this afternoon. I'll call you later.' As his dad's voice's trailed off to Percy Grainger's tune, Nick wondered if he was doing the right thing, but the thought of beach walks, bracing sea air and pints of Adnams

Broadside imbibed at his favourite watering hole, the Ship in Westlemere, convinced him it was the right thing to do.

Ben was taken aback. 'That's a bit out of the blue, Dad? You're not going to flee the country?'

'Of course not.'

'Perhaps you ought to give me your passport. Don't want you to be a fugitive on top of everything else.'

'I am not going on the run – tempting as it sounds. Will you be all right holding the fort?'

Ben grinned. 'Party time!'

Nick grimaced. 'Oh, and will you tell Grace where I am?'

'Me?'

'Tell her I'll call her from Grandpa's.'

Soon after Nick boarded the train at Liverpool Street an earnest young man with a Paisley print bucket hat and matching shorts greeted him with a 'Hi there, how are you doing?' Nick smiled politely back. 'It's me – Stevie.'

'I think you've made a mistake. You don't know me.'

'Yes I do,' the teenager responded amicably, 'And you know me.'

Nick doubted it. He had the sort of face that attracted attention from strangers – people would smile at him thinking they knew him. At petrol stations he would be greeted with a jolly 'Hello, Pete', or in the supermarket with an inquiring, 'How's it going, George?' When they discovered they didn't know him, they were greatly relieved. A woman in a top-notch restaurant once approached him to tell him, 'You look like my son.'

'Handsome fella?' Nick had replied.

'No!' the woman had shot back. 'Absolute cunt.'

This young man, however, wouldn't be put off, as though it was a game to make the journey go more quickly. 'Go on, try and remember.'

By now Nick was a little irritated. 'Look, you really don't know me. OK? I'm sure you're very nice, and in another life we might get on famously, but I've never set eyes on you in my life. Now could you please leave me alone?' And with that he made a great show of snapping open his laptop.

The young man got up and made to move down the carriage. He looked back and said, 'I'm a friend of Ben's. We've met a few times. Sorry to have bothered you.' With sudden regret Nick realised he did indeed know the young man and called out, 'Sorry, my mistake,' but Steve had already found a seat elsewhere. He'd have to square that with Ben next time they spoke.

Nick couldn't settle to his work, partly because he had so much on his mind, but also he was so easily distracted by everyone around him. He was always amazed that writers could work in cafés, trains or public places. Behind him an ageing couple dressed in black were clearly on their way to a funeral. He was reminded of a friend who worked in the registry office of the local council whose colleague, approached by members of the general public in floods of tears, would offer a stony-faced greeting of 'Birth, death or marriage?'

Across the aisle a white woman in dreadlocks a foot long (Ben wouldn't approve) had a brightly coloured tattoo of Noddy below one shoulder. No sign of Big Ears. Nick wondered idly whether this was discrimination against gnomes or just common sense. The badge she was wearing read, 'How dare you presume I have a pronoun.' He recalled Amy wearing a 'Women Are Magic' badge until he reminded her that Eva Braun was a woman.

The local train to Halesworth was always an enjoyable ride: Woodbridge, a picturesque market town eight miles from the North Sea, was the first stop, and Nick always found the glimpses of the harbour and its various boats strangely comforting. Between Wickham Market and Saxmundham he shifted his gaze from the window to stare at the elderly man sitting opposite. Nick stifled a laugh and then pretended to yawn, but the man had already noticed.

'Anything the matter?'

'No, not at all. Just a bit tired.'

'You were laughing at me. Go on, admit it.'

'No, no, no.'

'Tell me.'

'Well, I couldn't help but notice: you have an arrow drawn across your forehead.'

'What are you talking about?'

'In red. It's quite large.'

'Ah, they must have forgotten to remove it.'

Now Nick was curious. 'Who?'

'The medics. I had a skin blemish removed.'

'Oh, sorry to hear.'

'It's all fine.'

'I'm surprised nobody mentioned it.'

'Anyhow, thanks for telling me.' The man started furiously

rubbing his forehead with a handkerchief, producing a red glow across his forehead as though he was suffering from severe sunburn? 'Better?'

'Much,' Nick lied.

At Darsham his arrowed companion was replaced by a middle-aged tweedy woman, her dyed blonde hair neatly kept in place by an Alice band. She settled into her seat, produced a pair of miniature reading glasses and, to Nick's amazement, took out a copy of one of his earliest efforts, the vengeful and very unsuccessful autobiography of a tennis player entitled *Best Served Cold*.

Nick emitted a theatrical cough. 'Excuse me, I couldn't help but notice you're reading one of my books.'

The woman looked up. 'I beg your pardon?'

'I'm the author. That's my name on the cover. I'm Nick Greenwood.'

'Oh.' The woman studied the front cover. 'I've never met an author before. Would you sign it for me?'

'Of course.' It was moments like this that made his day. Sometimes it was lovely to be able to call yourself a writer.

'It isn't very good, actually. I got it at the library. It was in a pile they were giving away. I probably won't finish it but, now I've met you, my husband might be interested.'

She produced a pen and Nick reluctantly added his moniker to the title page. 'Did you know I only receive about ten pence each time one of my books is taken out? Can I suggest next time you buy one of my books?'

'Oh, I doubt there'll be a next time.'

The rest of the journey was spent in awkward silence. At Halesworth the woman left his book on the seat. He picked it up thinking he could always sell it, but then decided to leave it in place for the next lucky passenger.

Richard Greenwood was waiting for him in the station car park, and Nick braced himself for the eight-mile journey to Westlemere. His father had once been something of a boy racer, but an increasing lack of confidence in his motoring skills — always denied — now saw him drive so slowly that he had been stopped a number of times by police on the A12 for 'not keeping up with the traffic'. Nick thought it wasn't exactly dangerous driving, as if he did hit another vehicle the impact would be so light no damage would be incurred. Even if he ran into a pedestrian, it was more likely the car would be worse off. At some stage Nick knew he would have to tell his dad it was time for him to stop driving, but now he just wanted to get to his father's cottage in one piece.

After much manoeuvring in the driveway Nick finally felt safe enough to release his seat belt, and Richard suggested a cup of tea.

'Actually, Dad, are you up for a walk to the pub?'

'Splendid idea. I'll bring my stick. Not that I need it — it's just for effect.'

Soon after they had embarked on the short walk to the Ship, Richard Greenwood stopped in his tracks. 'Look at that sky.'

Nick nodded. 'Suffolk is so much about the sky.'

'I must disagree,' Richard said. 'It's not just about the sky.

I love being near the sea, and in the autumn when the heather comes out everywhere, it's absolutely glorious.'

'I love it here too, Dad.'

Richard stopped for a moment and spread out his arms. 'I wish your mother had been here to share this. I still miss her, Nick.'

Nick put an arm around his father. 'I know, Dad. Me too.'

'Although I have to say, I'm pleased she never knew about me squandering all that money. She worked so hard in that school for years. I was such a fool. She'd never have forgiven me.'

'Yes, she would, Dad. You were together a long time.'

'Not long enough ... And then there was Christopher ...' Richard Greenwood's voice trailed off.

Nick still found the death of his baby brother very difficult, even after all these years, and had always tried to avoid any discussion about his brother. But now felt he owed it to his father to engage with him. 'I can't imagine what you and Mum must have gone through. Losing a child ... I can't imagine losing Ben.'

'And you were so sweet then. Whenever we were watching television and there was a baby on the screen you stood in front of the set. It always reduced us to tears. And then you thought it was your fault that you'd made us unhappy.'

'I didn't know what to do.'

'We never got over his death or spoke about what happened. But we had you.' Richard turned to face his son. 'Ben's OK, isn't he?'

'Ben is fine,' said Nick. 'No need to worry about him.'

'So what brings you here?' Before Nick could answer, his dad said, 'It's lovely to see you, Nick, but you're not prone to sudden visitations. Something must be up.'

'Dad, I just wanted to catch up, it's been a while since I saw you and—'

'Come on, Nick. Spill the beans.'

Nick was surprised at his father's perception. 'Well. There are a few things that are worrying me at the moment.'

'Go on.' Richard prodded his son in the stomach with his stick. Why was it that elderly people always felt inclined to use their stick as a weapon?

Nick stared at his dad and knew he might as well come clean. 'I'm confused about a relationship, I've got health, work and money problems, and I'm under investigation for a murder. Well, two, actually.'

Richard stopped in his tracks, aghast. 'Good God, don't scare me like that. I know you have a rather warped sense of humour, but I really don't think that's very funny.'

'Dad, I'm not joking – about any of it. But please don't worry. It will all be fine.'

Richard stared at Nick, 'This is, this is . . . I don't know what to say. What are you going to do?'

'I don't know, Dad. It's mainly out of my hands. But please don't worry.'

'Well, I will of course, but I'm pleased you've come here.'

'I wanted to tell you in person, and I thought a few days away from it all in the country might help. You know, tramping across shingle beaches. The bracing air. Losing myself in Dunwich Forest.'

Nick's mobile vibrated. It was a text from Frankie.

We got it together and we're on tour. We fired Bruce and replaced him with Jim. Karen got us a few dates. Bless her. Enjoying being back on the road. I've decided to give the book another go, but it's pretty busy, so not sure I'll have much time for any writing in the next few months. Frankie

Ben was lying on his bed studying his mobile when Danesh knocked and entered immediately. 'I need to talk to you, Ben.' He glanced over Ben's shoulder. Ben's attempt to close the screen wasn't speedy enough. 'Are you looking at women, Ben?'

'Yes – but it's not what you—'

'You dirty devil!'

'Where did you learn that?'

'*Minder.*'

'It's not porn. I'm on Double Pivot.'

'I have never heard of this.'

'It's a dating app.'

'You are flicking the screen when you like the look of a girl?' Danesh gave Ben a look of approval. 'Amazing.'

'But it's not how she looks. There's more to it than that. We put on our interests, politics, ambitions. It's important not to view women just for their looks.'

'Why?'

'Why? From photographs you can't tell what a person is really like. Women have been objectified throughout history. You must have heard of toxic masculinity?'

'Is this an illness?'

'It's about the way men treat women. Male aggression, controlling behaviour, power.'

Danesh looked doubtful. 'I'm sure you are very nice to women.'

Ben nodded. 'I would be, given half the chance.'

'You have never had a girlfriend?'

'Yes, of course, but they didn't work out, and there's no-one at the moment.'

'No women at university?'

'Of course, but I don't want to hassle them.'

'What about your friends? Don't they have sisters?'

'That would be useful,' Ben admitted. 'But it could get complicated.'

'I see.' Danesh didn't see at all, but realised he had gone as far as he could without further embarrassing Ben.

'What was it you wanted to talk to me about?'

'Elysha is coming over later.'

That's nothing new, Ben thought. The two of them had been seeing a lot of each other recently. 'Cool.'

'We have plans.'

'What sort of plans?'

'Wedding plans. We are getting married.'

'*What?*' Ben almost dropped his phone.

'Elysha and I are getting married.' Danesh grinned.

Ben shook his head in disbelief. 'Bit soon, isn't it? You've only known each other for a few weeks.' Ben suddenly realised he wasn't pleased for Danesh, he was actually envious. In fact, very jealous. 'Isn't this more a marriage of convenience?' he added hopefully.

'I told Grace last week. She thinks I have got a good case, but said this might help.'

'I'm against arranged marriages in principle because the women don't get a choice,' said Ben.

'But you think this is a good idea?' Danesh paused. 'With Elysha?'

Ben hesitated. 'Well, I'm not sure—'

'You can come to the wedding. It's next week. Now you must get back to Double Pivot.' Danesh leant over to look at Ben's screen. 'She looks very lovely. Swipe for her, my friend.'

Nick had managed to avoid telling his father the full details of his current plight and Richard, to protect himself, hadn't asked. The day after Nick arrived in Suffolk, the two of them went to see the Ketts, hoping to put Cecil off the idea of a book without upsetting him. They were greeted somewhat frostily, the couple complaining that they hadn't heard from Richard recently and not at all from Nick.

Nick held his hands up. 'I've been pretty busy, and I'm really not sure I can take this project on. Certainly not at the moment.'

'There isn't much we can do until you've been to the Golden Eagle pow-wow at Easter and done a bit more research,' added Richard.

'Ha! That's where you're wrong,' Cecil replied. 'I've already been to New Mexico.'

'Really?' Nick was taken aback.

'I couldn't wait to get started, so I went to meet my tribe. We both went, didn't we, Gladys?'

'Well, I wasn't happy about Cecil going on his own — what with all those half-naked squaws.'

'If only,' Cecil dared to say under his breath. 'They treated us like royalty,' he continued. 'The elders taught me all about the great myths. I'm more determined than ever to take up my responsibilities. Someone to carry on the great tribal dynasty. I've already learned so much about the folklore and legends passed down from father to son.'

'Or daughter.' Nick thought Ben would approve of this addition.

'I need to record it all. But I'm no writer. That's where I need your help, Nick.'

'I'm impressed, Cecil, but the thing is, we haven't discussed a fee. I will need some money up front.' Nick was certain this would be the end of the matter.

'Not a problem. How much?'

Nick wasn't expecting this so, off the top of his head, said, 'Ten thousand pounds.'

'What?' Gladys was horrified.

Cecil was undeterred. 'Like I said, not a problem. Ten grand it is. I didn't tell you, old girl, that I snuck off one evening with a few of the boys to the Defeated Nations casino on the reservation and won twenty-five thousand dollars at roulette.'

Gladys was stunned into silence, while Nick was cross with himself that he hadn't asked for more.

'Roulette?' Richard was amazed. 'The Great Spirit was

certainly smiling on you that night. Did you use Native American sacred numbers?'

'No, I used my and Glad's birthdates. And then I stopped while I was ahead.'

Gladys shook her head in disbelief before giving Cecil a hug. 'You never fail to surprise me, Cecil Kett.'

Nick exchanged glances with his father. 'Well, like I've always said, it is a wonderful story. It would be an honour to take this on, Cecil.'

'Are you going to work on this together with your dad?'

Richard looked expectantly at his son.

'It will be a first, but yes. Why don't we, Dad?'

'I would love that, Nick. I would really love that.'

'You look sharp, boss.' Bogdan raised both thumbs. 'Very lemon tart.'

Leon looked askance at Bogdan. 'What are you talking about?'

'I start to learn rhyming slang, my old China. Lemon tart – smart.'

In full evening dress, Charlie Robertson was admiring himself in the colossal mirror that dominated the lounge. 'Not bad for a man of my age.'

Bogdan and Leon shot each other surreptitious glances.

'Very good, boss.'

'Amazing, Mr Robertson.'

'Right, I haven't called you just to play nice with me. Sit down, lads.' Leon and Bogdan made themselves comfortable on the white leather couch. 'I need to have a word with you about Steve Moran.'

Leon shook his head and removed his LA Dodgers baseball cap in a show of respect. 'One of them things.'

Bogdan followed suit with his woollen beany. 'Very bad. Very bad.'

Charlie snorted. 'I'll say it was very bad. You two really fucked up.'

Both henchmen stared at their feet.

'What did you two tell the Old Bill?'

'Nothing!' Bogdan nodded triumphantly. 'I plead the Fifth Amendment.'

Charlie raised his eyes heavenwards. 'No, you didn't, you berk.'

'We said we was nowhere near the scene,' said Leon. 'Although the CCTV picked us up.'

'But they didn't see us with Moran,' Bogdan added. 'And there were no witnesses.'

'They asked if Nick Greenwood had paid us to rough Moran up.'

'We said no.'

'We like to tell the truth.'

'My name didn't come up?'

'No, guvnor.' Leon thought it best to be economical with the truth.

'Good. That's something. Well, they won't get far with me.' Charlie paused. 'Anyway, I've got another job for you. I would appreciate if you were a little less heavy-handed.'

Leon perked up. 'What is it, boss?'

'It's about Ashley. Turns out Nick Greenwood hasn't found

out anything. Yeah, well, it was a fuck-up, and now he's had his collar felt it's down to you two.'

'Boss, it did seem a fucking stupid idea.'

'Language, Bogdan! *Language!* You're right, he was fucking useless. I want you two to follow her. But stay out of sight. I don't want her to think I'm suspicious of her.'

'But you are, boss.'

'I am not suspicious, Boggy, I'm just *inquisitive*. Acting as a concerned parent. Seeing as her mother is on the Costa and doesn't give a toss. Ashley's all I've got – well, apart from my other kids who I never see, even though I gave them everything they could want.' The lads looked suitably circumspect. 'It's a simple job,' Charlie went on. 'But don't let her see you.'

'Don't worry, boss,' said Bogdan. 'We keep our minces open.'

The second evening in Suffolk, Nick found himself back in the Ship as part of his dad's pub quiz team, the Amazing Avocets. The team consisted of local 'sparks' Brian Pope, retired postmaster Wilfred Bash, who wore a badge with the slogan, *Don't ask me to hurry – I'm from Suffolk*, to which Wilfred's erstwhile customers could certainly attest, and Billy Foster, delivery driver. Nick's attempt to point out the lack of women in the team had been quickly shot down by Wilfred. 'We tried it once, but it didn't work out.'

When Nick had inquired why, Brian Pope had mumbled, 'Bit of a know-all, if I recall.'

'Isn't that what you want in a—?' But Nick had been stopped in mid-flow by the stern faces all staring at Wilfred Bash. There was clearly some subtext it would be unwise to pursue.

Brian Pope turned to Nick. 'Did you know your dad has applied to be a lifeboat volunteer?'

'Really, Dad?'

'It's true, Nick. I wanted to be a crew member. I went down to the station, but they told me I had to be under sixty-five. Cheek.'

'Dad, I have to say, if I was caught in a gale and drifting in the North Sea, I'd rather have someone a bit fitter than you.'

'But the RNLI have given me an important position. I'm going to be a collector on flag days.'

'Good for you, Richard. You could make yourself a tidy sum.' Wilfred laughed at his own joke. No-one else did.

The quizmaster switched on his microphone. 'Well, I hope you're all ready for the second half of the quiz? I trust you've downed a few pints. I'm on a percentage.' There were a few half-hearted cheers.

Billy groaned, 'If he says that again next week . . .'

'This round is on sport. Question number one: who was beaten by Arthur Ashe in the 1975 Wimbledon final?'

'Ahh, I know this.' Nick raised his hand confidently. 'It was Jimmy Connors.'

'Oh, I don't think so,' Wilf piped up. 'John McEnroe, I reckon.'

'Don't be daft. He played much later. Pete Sampras?'

'No, Billy, you're wrong there.' Brian Pope was adamant. 'They weren't all American at Wimbledon.'

'You're right, it was an Australian. Lleyton Hewitt.'

Richard threw his hands up in the air. 'I'm afraid I haven't a clue. Unless it was Bobby Riggs?'

'Oh yes, the transgender bloke.'

Nick raised his voice above his team-mates' discussion. 'That was Renée Richards, who never played in a Wimbledon final. Listen, I was there. It was Jimmy Connors.'

'Sure?'

Nick raised his voice. 'Yes, Dad. I queued up all night. It was definitely Jimmy Connors!'

Billy raised a finger to his lips. 'You're giving the answer away to the other teams.'

'But if you don't think I'm right, what does it matter?' Nick put his head in his hands.

The Avocets' discussion was interrupted by the quizmaster. 'Question two. The 1923 Cup Final was known as the White Horse Final, but who was the victorious team?'

As the team embarked on another tortuous discussion, Nick's mobile rang.

'You can't use a mobile during the quiz,' said Wilf.

The call was from Grace. 'Sorry, guys.' Nick made his way to the Gents.

'Hi Grace, is everything all right?'

'That's what I was going to ask you. You left without saying goodbye. And after everything you told me. I didn't know what to think.'

'I asked Ben to tell you I was here.'

'He did. He said you would call me.'

'I meant to. But then I didn't think you'd want to have anything to do with me. I'm sorry, Grace, I'm not handling this very well. I needed to get away for a few days. It was all getting a bit much.'

'Nick, running away from all this isn't going to help!' There was a pause. 'Nick, why are you whispering? And there's someone shouting in the background.'

'He's the quizmaster.'

'What?'

'The quizmaster. I'm in the pub with Dad and a few of his friends and I'm not meant to be on the phone.'

'Can't you go outside?'

'No, they'll think I'm googling some answers. I'm having to pretend I'm not feeling very well. Are the boys OK?'

'They're fine. In fact, Danesh and Ben are becoming good friends. When are you coming back, Nick?'

'Soon.'

'Good. I miss you.'

'And I miss you, Grace. I think I'm in love with you.'

'When will you know?'

'Umm . . . listen, I think the quizmaster's onto me. I'd better go.'

'Promise me you'll video-call me tonight. I'd like to see your face.'

'I promise, Grace. One more thing.'

'Yes?'

'You don't happen to know who won the 1923 FA Cup Final?'

Charlie Robertson had been drying off on his lounger after his 20 lengths when Bogdan and Leon had turned up to explain the results of their travails.

'OK, I'm with you so far, Leon. You followed Ashley into Camden Town?'

'Yes, Mr Robertson. She was in an Uber.'

'An Uber? What the fuck was she doing in an Uber?' Charlie furiously towelled himself down. 'Was she with anyone?'

'A couple of friends.'

'Men or women?'

'Women. Very glamorous, weren't they, Bogman?'

'Very beautiful. All three of them. And very well dressed.'

'Then what?'

'She went into the Town Hall.'

'The Town Hall? Was she paying a fine?'

'Dunno, boss.'

'You didn't follow her in there?'

'No, Mr Robertson. You told us not to be seen.'

'Then what?'

'Well, we waited half an hour and—'

'Yes?'

Leon and Bogdan exchanged glances. 'She came out with a man,' said Leon.

'A man.'

'That's what I said, boss.'

'Maybe he was her brief?'

'They were kissing,' added Bogdan. 'Weren't they, Leon?'

Charlie was stumped. 'Well, that couldn't have been her brief. Although you never know with some of these lawyers.'

'They looked very happy.' Bogdan nodded in agreement.

Charlie was dumbfounded. 'So that's it?'

'No. We watched them go into a pub with their friends.'

'That's all you've got? It doesn't explain what she's been up to all this time.'

'Perhaps she go there every day?' Bogdan suggested helpfully.

'Why would she go to the Town Hall every day, you clown? You think she's got a job on the council?'

Leon shrugged. 'Do you want us to follow her again today?'

Charlie threw his towel down with an angry flourish. 'No, it's too late. She said she was going away for a couple of days with a friend. I'm going to have to ask her face to face. Subterfuge and subtlety were never my strong points.'

'As Micky Mellon found to his cost,' muttered Leon.

Charlie executed an almost perfect swallow dive into the deep end.

14

Nick and Richard were sitting on a bench at Halesworth Station.

'It's a shame you're leaving so soon.'

'It's been a nice break, Dad. Pleased to see you looking so well.' Staying with his father for a few days had made Nick realise his father wasn't losing it; just that Richard's eccentricities had become accentuated. 'And winning the pub quiz was the highlight of my year.'

'Exactly! Who knew that a snail can sleep for three years. And it's illegal to tip waiters or waitresses in Japanese restaurants. Or was it that you can't tip anyone in a Japanese restaurant if you have octopus? Anyway, extraordinary what you can learn at a pub quiz.'

Nick put his arm round his dad's shoulder. 'I need to get back to Ben.'

'And anyone else?' Despite Nick's attempts at secrecy, Richard hadn't failed to notice the regular phone calls to Grace.

'Yes. There is someone else. I'm missing her more than I thought.'

'Glad to hear it. Don't waste any more time. She might find

someone else. Do you know I nearly lost your mother to an artist I introduced her to?'

'You had a love rival, Dad?'

'I was trying to play it cool, and Felix John was devilishly handsome, called himself a "post-modernist", which for some reason she initially found alluring. But your mother couldn't resist my—'

'Dad, I don't think I need to know — oh, look, train's coming.' Nick was saved further embarrassment by the arrival of the 11.25 to Ipswich.

'Nicholas, you haven't really told me what really is going on in your life.'

'Well, I thought you would only worry. I will in time, Dad. I promise.'

'I'll leave it to you.' Richard gave his son an awkward hug.

'Thanks for having me, Dad. It has helped. And we've got Cecil's book to work on.'

'Indeed we have. But before you go I want you have to have this. I haven't really known what to do with it for all these years.' Richard handed Nick a crumpled Hamleys plastic bag that he had been clutching tightly. 'I want you to have it.' Nick reached inside and pulled out his brother's teddy bear.

Sam Goldman had decided to see how Kitty was settling in at Footlights House, and hoped he would find her relaxed and recovering from her hospital stay. Unfortunately, the place was in turmoil. There were rumours that Harold Williams, a well-known entertainment and theatre critic, had been admitted to the home. A small crowd had gathered in the lounge, where murmurings of discontent in stage whispers circulated. Several residents, including Kitty, were up in arms, and had produced newspaper cuttings of terrible reviews Williams had written about them, which surprisingly they had kept:

> As Vladimir he was so dull, I wasn't surprised Godot didn't turn up.
>
> Her accent wavered from Newcastle to Belfast and ended somewhere between Birmingham and Bath.
>
> It was less a coming-of-age performance than the arrival of infirmity.
>
> Her best moments were when she was offstage.

'Who'd ever want to become a critic?' Vernon Barrett called out.

'No-one,' they chorused.

'Has anybody seen a drama critic in the daytime?' Sam chipped in. 'Of course not. They come out after dark, up to no good.' He looked to Kitty for a response.

'That's very good, Sam.'

Edward Harcourt smiled kindly. 'That's P. G. Wodehouse, isn't it?'

'I was about to mention that.'

Harry Hallyday wheeled himself to the table. 'What's the matter with you lot? I've had some terrible notices – you can't be bitter in this business. I felt like committing suicide once, although if I had done myself in, I might have lived to regret it.'

Teddy Harcourt was waving a yellowing piece of newspaper. 'Here's one for you, Harry: "His material was as funny as a shark attack, but without the teeth."'

'Who was the comic?'

'You, Harry.'

'Bloody hell! We can't let him in here.'

Winifred Bates was trying to allay their fears. 'Mr Williams is only coming for a visit. It's not definite that he'll be admitted.'

'It's definite that he won't be admitted.' Vernon Barrett produced a review from 1964. '"Vernon Barrett was more wooden than the New Forest."'

'You'll have to excuse us, Mr Goldman,' Winifred Bates said. 'We've also we had a resident pass away this morning, so everyone is in a bit of state.'

'Oh dear, I'm sorry to hear that.'

By way of explanation the matron added, 'She had breathing difficulties.'

'Yes, that was her main difficulty,' agreed Harry. 'She stopped breathing.' He removed his Panama theatrically. 'Dolly Rogers, the most ancient soubrette in the business. Poor old girl. No longer *Hello, Dolly*. It's more like *Goodbye, Dolly*.'

Sam winced, but this did nothing to deter Hallyday. 'I did have a soft spot for her. I once gave her an X-ray of my chest for her birthday – wanted to show her my heart was in the right place.'

Teddy Harcourt could bear no more quips from the ageing comic, whose material was older than Harry himself. A swift departure was required and, much to Sam and Kitty's relief, Teddy led them into the dining room, where they found a corner table. Teddy gazed affectionately at Kitty, took her hand in his and then drew it to his lips.

Kitty withdrew her hand in mock embarrassment. 'I've been thinking a lot about this,' she said, turning to Sam. 'You'll be glad to know I've decided to stay at Footlights House. The fact that Teddy is here has made all the difference.'

Sam smiled. 'So it seems. Well, I'm delighted, for both of you. It appears you have a fairytale ending for your book.'

'Quite. And a little ironic. It was partly through Nick Greenwood that I ended up here with Teddy. Do you know he rang me earlier to see how I was? He told me he often looked at a photograph I gave him of my grandfather and thought about the story I had told him. Said how much it had helped him. I don't know what he was talking about.'

Frankie was supping a pint in an alcove at the Canal Hotel. 'How are things? How's the family?'

Small talk was not one of Frankie's hobbies, and it immediately put Nick off his guard. 'Fine, thanks.'

'Listen, Nick, I've got some news.'

'Penned a paragraph or two, have you?'

'I've formed a new band, Aslan Resurrected, and we've only gone and got a gig at fucking Glastonbury.'

'Oh, that's great news.' Nick was genuinely pleased. 'How did that happen?'

'Karen turned out to be a great manager. Surprisingly well

connected, although we still have to listen all that bible-bashing from her and Harvey. Not the main stage, of course.'

'Of course not.'

'The Corner Flag stage.'

'Not heard of that one.'

'On the edge of the campground. The thing is' – Frankie took a long sip from his Guinness – 'as well as giving Bruce the heave-ho, I'm also going to have to let you go.'

Nick sat up straight. 'Pardon?'

'Yeah. I've employed a new ghostwriter.'

'A new ghostwriter?'

'I don't think we gelled. Didn't feel right. I felt there was something missing.'

'What was missing was some bloody work from you.'

'Dave and Den agree with me.'

'Who?'

'The guys that were here last time.'

'What's it got to do with them?'

They're fans. They know me. Better than you.'

'Frankie, we've been working together for *months*. Well, I say *we* . . . and I say *working* . . .'

'Also I don't feel I can trust you.'

'*Trust me*? Trust me with what? You haven't told me anything.'

'I've kept all our conversations on my mobile, and when I played them back I felt you weren't properly listening, man. I mean, listen to this.' Frankie switched his mobile to speakerphone.

'So, Frankie, what can you tell me about your time at art college?'
'I never went to art college. You must be thinking of someone else.'

Nick was bemused, 'But I'm sure you told me—'
'Here's another one.'

''I don't want you to go anywhere near Steve Moran. You understand me?'
'What do you say, Bogman?'
'Sure, Leon. Whatever Mr Greenwood say.'
'I mean it, both of you. I don't want anything to happen to him.'

Nick stared at Frankie. 'You've got that conversation on your phone?'

'I've got an app which records all my conversations.'

'Because you don't trust me?'

'It's not just you I don't trust. I don't trust anyone. Except for Lucy.'

'So you have a recording of that conversation?'

'Sounds like it, doesn't it?' Sometimes Frankie couldn't believe how dim Nick could be.

Nick was stunned. He looked at Frankie in disbelief. 'You realise that this will clear me?'

What *was* Nick talking about? Now Frankie was certain he'd done the right thing. His ghostwriter had clearly lost his marbles.

'You've got come with me to the police station – *now*!'

'No way, man! I was meant to report to one in 1993 and never turned up – they might keep me there.'

'This is important! My life depends on you helping me! Please, Frankie! It's the last thing I'll ask of you. I can explain on the way.'

Even if Nick had gone completely nuts, after all they'd been through he thought he owed his ghostwriter this favour. He grasped Nick's arm. 'If I'm not back by six, man, Luce will give me hell.'

Nick greeted Sergeant Finchley with a cheerful, 'Show me your finest suite.'

'You're asking to go into custody, sir?'

'Not exactly.'

Sergeant Finchley turned to DC Martin, who was immersed in paperwork. 'Mr Greenwood is giving himself up.'

'No, I'm not.' Nick was triumphant. 'I'm actually here to clear my name.' Nick turned to a bemused Frankie.

'Blimey!' Sergeant Finchley did a double take. 'It's Frankie Morrison!'

Frankie turned to leave. 'I knew it. I'm still on the wanted list.'

'I'm a great fan of yours,' Finchley beamed.

Frankie stopped in his tracks. 'What?'

'Aslan are one of my favourite bands.'

WPC Mackenzie had joined the gathering.

'Lovely to see you again, Susy,' said Nick. 'If I may call you that?'

In the interviewing room Nick said, 'Wait till you hear this. Go on, Frankie.'

Frankie tapped 'Play', and the four of them listened intently to the recording of the phone call between Frankie and Nick in which Nick instructed Bogdan and Leon not to go anywhere near Steve Moran. DC Martin looked at WPC Mackenzie, who looked at Frankie, who turned to Nick, who smiled triumphantly at DC Martin.

'And you can verify this is a legitimate recording of a phone call you had with Mr Greenwood?'

'I can give you the date.' Frankie beamed at the two police officers.

DC Martin shrugged at Nick. 'Well, this may well help your case, but it's not definitive. You may have changed your mind. And it does prove you know Bogdan Dimitrescu and Leon King, who we've interviewed in connection with the death of Steve Moran. It's not the end of the matter.'

'But I've never denied knowing them. In any case, you let them go. And so now I can walk out of here a free man?'

'When we have spoken to you about something else.'

'Please tell me,' Nick said wearily.

'You may want to discuss this in private with us. Not in front of Mr Morrison.'

'It's all right. I have no secrets from Frankie.'

'It's about your wife.'

'Ex-wife.'

'There was no post-mortem following her death.'

'That's because—'

'And we were unable to exhume the body to perform another post-mortem.'

'And that's because—'

'Mr Greenwood, please.' DC Martin was growing impatient. 'Because she was cremated.'

'That's what I tried to tell you before.'

'So we are not pursuing the matter any further.' WPC Mackenzie seemed almost relieved.

'And that's all you were going to do?' Nick asked.

'Was there another line of enquiry we should be following?' inquired DC Martin.

'No, not at all.' Nick thought he'd better shut up now. 'I'm very grateful. For your help, that is.' He turned to a bewildered Frankie. 'Come on – let's go.'

'What the fuck was that all about?'

'I'll tell you one day, Frankie.'

The desk sergeant stopped Frankie. 'Mr Morrison! Could I have your autograph?'

Nick couldn't wait to get out of the police station, so left the two men in animated conversation. While awaiting his Uber, he saw Frankie climb into the front seat of an unmarked police car, driven by Sergeant Finchley. Still, Frankie had certainly got Nick off the hook. Yesterday he'd been in the frame for two murders; now he was a free man.

On the way home his euphoria was tempered by a text message advising him to contact the hospital urgently as the results were 'in'. Whoever had written that message, Nick decided, had been watching a little too much *Strictly Come Dancing*.

'Mr Greenwood, you'll be glad to know that there is no trace of the disease in the bone.'

Nick put his head in his hands, overcome with emotion and initially unable to speak. When he did look up at Dr Hanson, all he could utter was a whispered, 'Thank you.'

Dr Hanson smiled at him. 'I'm pleased for you. It is good news.'

'And now what?' Nick dared to ask.

'Well, regular checks, and you will need to continue with the hormone treatment.'

'For how long?'

'For the foreseeable future.'

'And what about sex?'

'Well, I've got another patient in fifteen minutes.'

Nick looked at Dr Hanson in amazement.

'Sorry, couldn't resist, Mr Greenwood. I'm asked that question so many times, and you are a man with a well-developed sense of humour.'

'Dr Hanson, I'm surprised at you.'

Dr Hanson blushed.

'Still, you delivered it nicely. Anyway: what about sex in the future?'

'As I think you've been told, I'm afraid a loss of libido is very likely and' – Dr Hanson pursed her lips and nodded dramatically – 'there will be some shrinkage.'

Junior Hamilton was about to start a punditry session on Sky Gillette Soccer Saturday when he received a video call. 'Hi Junior, it's Clarissa. I've got some good news.'

'Look, if you want to come back to me, it's no good, Clarissa. Junior Hamilton only gets dumped once. In any case I've met someone else. She plays for Chelsea – we're much better suited. And she appreciates my charity–'

'All pending lawsuits have been dropped.'

'What?'

'Your book. No-one wants to sue any more. Seems the publisher hired a hotshot lawyer who put the fear of God into all of them. That Nobby Smith player was the first. They found all sorts of stuff on him.'

'Oh.' Junior paused. 'Cool. I suppose.'

'And, Junior...'

'What?'

'I'm pleased for you. Honestly. Bye.' The last thing Junior saw of Clarissa was her blowing him a farewell kiss.

'Deirdre, you look terrible.'

'I'm sorry, Nick. I left it as long as I could, but I was in a bit of a state, couldn't sleep – couldn't concentrate on anything. But I finally spoke to my supervisor. I'm afraid I have to inform the police about your murders.'

Nick leaned back in his chair. 'No, you don't.'

'Nick, I do. Supposing you killed someone else? And what about my professional reputation?'

'I have no intention of killing or arranging to kill anyone.'

'Oh, Nick, if only that was true.'

Nick sat up in mock horror. 'Deirdre – you don't trust me?'

'Well, you did confess that you murdered Amy.'

Nick smiled. 'Let me put you out of your misery. I've been cleared of involvement in both deaths.'

Deirdre threw her notebook across the room. The print of *The Scream* came crashing down, sending glass everywhere. 'Why the fuck didn't you tell me before?'

'I've only just found out. By the way, I'm glad to see the back of that poster.' A thought suddenly hit Nick. 'You didn't give your supervisor my name?'

'No, it's all confidential.'

'Oh, and the other good news is that the cancer hasn't spread, and I should respond to the hormone treatment.'

A stunned Deirdre was slowly recovering. 'And don't tell me world peace has also been declared. Well, that is all amazing.'

'I know.'

'What about Grace? Have you told her everything?'

'Yes. But there is *one* more thing I need to tell her.'

'Nick, don't keep me in suspense!'

'Sorry, Deirdre. Time's up.'

15

At 'Tu Lions', Charlie Robertson's birthday party was in full swing. In the ballroom, a band was playing a selection of show tunes and hits from the 1960s while Leon was mixing potent cocktails, which Bogdan and some hired staff were distributing to the guests. A gaggle of sharply dressed men in the kitchen were discussing the venue for their next 'golf game' and Shazza Robertson, squeezed into a skin-tight, zebra-pattern onesie, was in particularly garrulous mood. She'd been at the prosecco since 5 o'clock, greeting each guest with, 'You look amazing, darling,' 'Where did you get that frock?' and 'Love that pout. New lips?' She cut dead Melanie, Fingers Chapman's ex-wife, however, after that unfortunate fracas at Stringfellows. She would have a word – and it wouldn't be quiet – with Charlie about how Melanie had got an invitation.

The curiously old-fashioned email invitation – 'Charlie Robertson will be at home' – had arrived the previous week. Despite being tempted to reply, 'And so will Nick Greenwood', Nick received a follow-up telephone call from Charlie insisting that he bring family members and any number of friends and 'kiddies'. 'It ain't a party unless I have at least a couple of hundred guests. Nick, you won't want to miss this. The last one, we had to throw out at least ten drunks.'

An initially reluctant Grace, urged on by Ben, who was keen to meet a real gangster, had agreed to accompany Nick. Marcel – never one to pass on a party – made it abundantly clear that he wasn't going to miss out on the fun: 'Obviously I'm going. Completely.' The four of them had been collected by Leon, who was particularly careful in protecting Nick's head when manoeuvring him into the car. Leon greeted Grace with, 'You look gorge, darlin'.' Ben, who was about to say something about Leon's sexism, took one look at their over-muscled chauffeur and decided to keep quiet.

Charlie had ordered champagne cocktails for all of them, including Marcel – 'He looks like he can handle the hard stuff' – and Marcel wandered off to explore the house with Ben. 'This your lady friend?' Charlie asked Nick.

'This is Grace.'

'Enchanted.' Charlie took Grace's hand and kissed it and looked her up and down. 'Bit out of your league, ain't she, Nick?' Before either of them could respond, Charlie had squeezed Grace's hand and said, 'Get yourself another cocktail from Leon over there, sweetheart. I need to have a word with himself here. Won't keep him long.'

Grace was already frowning at Charlie's comments and being dismissed so perfunctorily, but a quick look from Nick told her she didn't have much choice.

Charlie turned to Nick. 'Sad about Steve Moran. Tragic, really. According to the papers he had so much to live for.'

'Mainly coughing up the money he owed me.'

'Yeah. That didn't quite work out as we'd hoped. Still, look on the bright side. We're all in the clear. All charges dropped, no witnesses. There never are with me.'

'Yes, I don't want to hear any more, Charlie. It's been a nightmare.'

'But I've got a bone to pick with you,' Charlie continued. 'You never did find out what my Ash has been up to, did you?'

'Well, I did try—'

'Never mind — we won't dwell. But she promised to be here tonight. So someone is going to have to ask her straight out. Aren't they, Nick? That's if you still want your dosh.'

Nick started to protest but Charlie placed his hand firmly on Nick's shoulder. 'No more apologies, sunshine. Now, 'scuse me, I have to say a few words to the assembled.'

Nick went in search of Grace and found her watching her son playing snooker with Ben, who was helping Marcel hold the cue correctly for fear of his charge ripping a huge tear in the green baize. When Marcel spotted Nick he broke off from the table, steered him next to Grace and placed his mother's hand in Nick's. 'That's b . . . better.'

'Marcel!' — Ben feigned exasperation — 'we're in the middle of a game!'

'G . . . g . . . go on, Mum,' Marcel urged. 'Kiss him!'

Grace's hands went to her hips. 'Marcel,' she said gently, 'you can't go around saying things like that.'

Marcel turned to Nick: 'You do it' – and pursed his lips and mimed the first passionate kiss he had seen Ross give Rachel in an episode of *Friends* he had watched numerous times. 'Did you know Mum loves you?'

'Does she?'

'She wants to marry you.'

Grace was horrified. 'I said no such thing!'

Marcel winked at Nick and returned to the snooker table. 'My turn, Ben?'

'—Your sister's on the roof and she won't come down.' The guests reacted with raucous laughter at the punchline of Charlie's favourite joke, despite the fact that they had heard him tell it many times. 'So all I need to say is thank you all for coming tonight. It's my birthday gift to you – my favourite people in all the world. Eat, drink yourselves silly and, oh, yeah, the pool is open for anyone who has brought a costume – and even for those who haven't.' The last remark elicited numerous '*Oy oy!*'s from the assembled gathering. 'Enjoy yourselves, stay as long as you like, but not beyond Wednesday when I'm playing golf.'

A few cheers and a smattering of applause greeted the end of the speech, at which point Charlie spotted his daughter Ashley making her arrival, hand in hand with a handsome man. He gave his daughter a fulsome hug. 'Hello, darling. You look beautiful!' He broke off his clinch to give her companion the once over. 'And who's this?'

'This is Danesh, Daddy. He's my husband.'

For about ten seconds Charlie was terrifyingly silent. 'Fucking hell, Ash. You having a laugh?'

Ashley shook her head. 'I've got a few things to tell you.'

Charlie was looking her companion up and down, which made Danesh smile nervously. 'Too right. Come into the study, Ash. You stay here, son.'

Father and daughter sat down on the velvet-covered chaise longue.

'How long have you known this geezer, Ash?'

'He's called Danesh. He's a refugee. He's been through terrible times, Daddy.'

'Haven't we all?'

'He's almost a doctor.'

'Yeah, and I was almost Liberace. You married him without telling me!' Suddenly Charlie looked small and old. 'That's what hurts, Ash. I wanted to walk you down the aisle! A proper church wedding with all my closest mates celebrating with me.' He was looking somewhere into the distance. 'We might have even asked your mother.'

'That was never going to happen, Daddy. I know it's a shock, but you'll get to like him.'

Charlie stared intently at his daughter. 'Do you love him, Ash?'

'Very much.'

'You know, you're all I've got, Ash. Your half-brothers and stepsisters won't give me the time of day. They're not even here tonight. I love you, sweetheart.'

'I know, Dad. I know. I love you too. I didn't mean to hurt you.' Tears began to flow down Ashley's cheeks. Then she composed herself again. 'There's more, Daddy.'

'You ain't up the duff?'

'I've been working as a glamour model on TV.'

'Jesus, what a birthday.' A sudden thought hit Charlie. 'Not naked?'

'Of course not! Bikinis, lingerie, that sort of thing. You can't reveal everything before the watershed.'

Charlie was still thinking. 'No wonder Nick didn't find out what you were doing during the day.'

'Who?'

'Nick Greenwood. My ghostwriter. I hired him to find out what you were up to.'

Ashley stared back at her father. 'That's bonkers, Dad. I went to him to help me with my book. But I never met him.'

'You actually went to his place, and he *still* couldn't trace you? Unbelievable!' Charlie furrowed his brow. 'Wait a minute. What do you mean, "my book"?'

'I've given up modelling now, Dad. I'm now a writer.'

'Strewth. This gets worse and worse.'

Just then Ben, who had been unsuccessfully searching for one of the several toilets, burst into the study. His eyes fell on Charlie. 'Oh, I'm really sorry, I was looking for the—' He stopped in his tracks. 'Elysha! What are you doing here?'

'Son, this is a private conversation between me and my daughter,' growled Charlie. 'And who's this Elysha?'

Ashley stood up. 'It's all right, Ben. I'll tell my dad everything. You'd better go.'

Ben exited muttering, 'I'd better tell *my* dad everything.'

Charlie gazed at his daughter. 'I think I need to have few more words with your new husband. But first, I think I'd like to share this news with my guests.'

While Ben was excitedly describing to an astonished Nick that Ashley and Elysha were the same person, in the ballroom Charlie was quietening down the crowd again. 'I thought I had finished my speech, but it seems that Ash has just married this fella here. Please raise your glasses to her and — what's his name, Ash?'

'Danesh.'

'Not only has she got married without me knowing, but she's been working as a glamour model. And now, she's taken up writing. And to think I always thought she would have a proper job.'

As soon as the band had begun to play again, Ashley, accompanied by a young woman, approached a still shaken Ben. 'All right?'

'Yes, it's all a bit of a shock.'

Ashley squeezed Ben's arm affectionately. 'Anyway, I want you to meet a friend of mine. This is Maya.'

Maya spread out both her hands to Ben, who grasped them self-consciously. 'Hi Maya. Pleased to meet you.' Ben had spotted Maya earlier. She had seemed not to know anyone and was sitting on one of the sofas looking a little lost. Ben would never admit to having a type, but if he did this girl would definitely have been his: tall, slim with styled, red hair, and very pretty in a natural sort of way. He had been tempted to talk to her, but didn't want to be thought of as a typical male predator. He couldn't believe his luck.

Ashley had spotted Charlie making a beeline for her new husband and hurried off after them.

'How do you know Elysha?' Ben asked Maya — 'I mean Ashley?'

'I'm a school friend. I'm a student.'

'Not a model?'

'Oh, no. Hope you're not disappointed?'

'Nooo — but you could be. I mean — if you wanted to be — because you're very ... I mean, there's nothing *wrong* with being a model, if that's what you choose to do ...'

Ben would later admit to Maya that her giggle was being the sexiest thing he'd ever heard. 'You're getting yourself in a right tangle, Ben. It's OK. I was hoping to meet you here.'

Ben couldn't believe his ears. 'Were you?'

'Ash has told me a lot about you. I know you had a bit of a crush on her, didn't you? Maybe still do?'

'I wouldn't say that.' Ben could feel his face redden.

'I'm afraid I can't stay long tonight.'

'Oh.' Ben didn't think he had ever been more disappointed in his whole life. 'No, it's not really my thing either.'

'Oh, it's not that,' said Maya. I'm going to a gig later. Ezra Collective.'

Ben's eyes lit up. 'Oh, I really wanted to go to that! Couldn't get a ticket.'

Maya smiled. 'I've got a spare if you're interested.'

While the two of them were gazing at each other, Marcel sidled up to Ben. 'Do you like her?'

'Er, we've only just met.'

'I think you like her. Are you going to m . . . marry her, Ben? She's fit. Definitely fit. Obviously.'

Maya giggled again. 'It's a bit early for that. Who are you?'

'Marcel. B . . . Ben's friend. P . . . p . . . pleased to meet you.' He looked up at Ben with a serious expression. 'But if you marry her, can we still play FIFA?'

Nick was recapping the events of the evening with Grace when he was interrupted by Bogdan. 'Mr Greenwood, I need to speak to you.'

'Yes, Bogdan?'

'I have fascinating story for you to write.'

'A lot of people say that to me.'

'Better than Charlie's. That was load of pony.'

'Oh, Bogdan.' Nick hesitated. 'I don't know. Do you have any money?'

Bogdan winked at Nick. 'I have plenty of money. We meet tomorrow. Yes?'

'I suppose I might be able to find the time.'

'Not tomorrow, Nick,' said Grace. 'It's Sunday. You and I are spending it together.'

'Are we?'

Grace took Nick by the arm and led him away from a bemused Bogdan to the edge of the bandstand. Nick turned to the Romanian and mimed making a phone call.

'Nick, I think we need to talk. Properly.'

'I agree,' Nick replied. 'We must.'

'I wasn't expecting that.' Grace was genuinely surprised.

'Grace, I have something to tell you. For quite a while now. I've been holding back for . . . oh, for a number of reasons.'

'Go on.'

'But first things first. Did you really tell Marcel you wanted to marry me?'

'Don't be ridiculous, Nick. What is this, the nineteen-fifties? Marcel's always wanting my single friends to get married. He's surprisingly traditional in that respect. He sometimes asks people about their prospects. I don't know where he got that from. A soap, I expect. Anyway, what was it you wanted to tell me, Nick?'

Nick scratched his head and mumbled, 'I love you, Grace.'

'Pardon?'

'I *love* you. I can't say it any louder. Do you want the whole room to know?'

'Maybe I do. But are you sure this time? You don't just think you do?'

'No, I'm pretty sure this time.'

'Mmm. Well, that sounds more encouraging. Then how about we make tomorrow a proper date?'

'Definitely.'

'And can you try not to be abducted by gangsters halfway through?'

'I'll do my best. But you never know with Charlie . . .'

'Oh, I'll tell him to leave us alone. I think he'll listen to me.'

Nick thought that was probably true.

'Now, it's not like I'm going to follow Marcel's suggestion, but exactly what are your prospects?'

'Ah. Not good.'

'Not very helpful. I need more.'

'Well, you know about my health, my limited earnings and that death seems to follow me around.'

Grace angled her head to one side. 'So that's the best you can offer? You can't have sex, you're broke, and then there are the murders.'

Nick shrugged. 'Oh, well. Nobody's perfect.'

The patient opens her eyes and stares up at the ceiling.

This is agony. How can she still be alive? Typical: he'd tried to keep his part of their agreement, but he'd fucked up. He hadn't even managed to finish her off, the damn fool. Now what? The awful existence she has endured for these past months will continue.

Half an hour later two nurses enter her room, and exchange glances.

One puts her hand on Amy's wrist. There is no pulse. 'Looks like she's had another stroke.' The nurse crosses herself. The other closes Amy's still-staring eyes.

Acknowledgements

First of all, huge thanks to my editor Graham Coster for his incredible diligence, skilful guidance and friendship.

Grateful appreciation to Peter Davison, who was involved at the inception of this book, and some of whose material I have borrowed shamelessly.

Advice has been gleaned from Professor Mervyn Singer OBE on some medical matters, and from Chris Miller on police procedures.

I am greatly indebted to family and friends for their encouragement in the writing of this novel during difficult times, but my old writing partner Peter Morfoot deserves a special mention.

A Very Special Thank You to my wife Alison Wellemin, who provided the cover illustration, support and love, although not necessarily in that order, and to my grown-up children Daniel, Sarah and Joel, for their enthusiastic participation and for inspiring several characters.